Phantoms Inc. ②

AND THE
CURSE OF THE DARK ORCHID

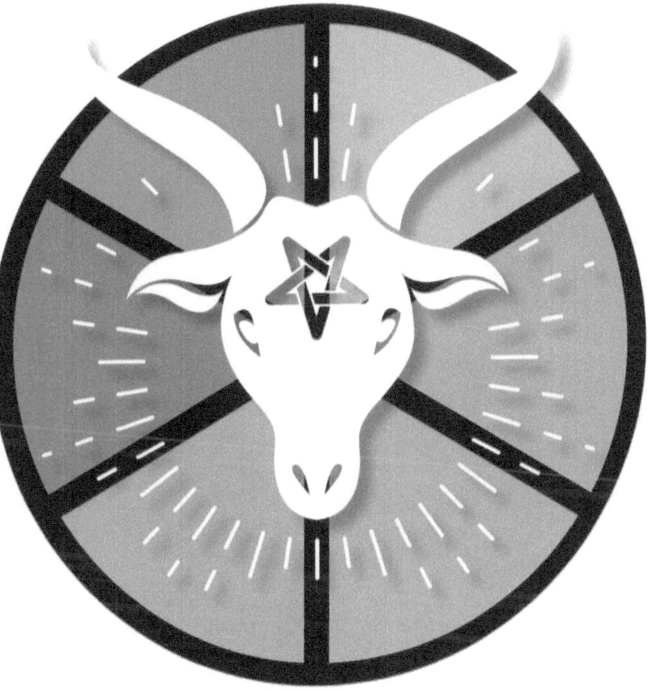

DARREN LEE FLOYD

ISBN: 978-1-8381611-6-3

Published by Stratosphere Books

Cover design & interior formatting:
Mark Thomas / Coverness.com

For my brother Mark, I'll always be in your corner.

PROLOGUE

Milán Crávthers gazed at the half-eaten apple and his stomach growled. The apple was among other scraps of food in a wooden box, which he was going to steal.

The old town square was a mixture of the Renaissance follies of a ruling family that had died out decades previously and the muddy, smelly realities of a busy working town. The only working sewage system was the nearby river, where families and businesses emptied their slop buckets. Vermin ran riot along the cobbled streets. When there was an easterly wind the town square would be filled with the stench of sulfur and human waste. Citizens of noble birth walked around with a small posy of flowers beneath their nostrils while everyone else had to get used to it.

Milán looked around and when he couldn't see his brother. He feared the worst. Had he been caught stealing? Had he been thrown into jail? Into the filth-clogged river? He didn't know what he'd do if his brother didn't come back. He'd be alone in this cold, harsh world. And the boy had more immediate worries. He ached with hunger and seeing the food outside the tavern made it worse. The old town square was busy, with merchants and horse-drawn carts going back and forth. Milán would use the activity as a cover to steal some food. They'd been chased away before and the tavern owner had threatened to cut their fingers off if he caught them again. The miserable fat miser, why did he care? He was fat enough! Milán was about to leap forward to snatch the food when he felt a hand on his shoulder.

"Here! I've brought you shoes!" His brother had two skins in his hand from an unrecognizable small animal. Maybe squirrels? They had been gutted and rudimentary holes been made in the skins with string threaded through.

"Thank you, brother." Milán tied them around his dirty, bloody feet.

Jan already had "shoes" but they already looked like they had been worn through. Their clothes were threadbare and completely worn through in places. Jan's trousers were actually an old coal sack with two holes poked through for legs and tied around his waist with rope to keep it up. It seemed that Jan had to pull the rope a little bit tighter every day. He wore an oversized coat—its origins lost in memory—which was stuffed with straw and newspaper, making him look like a boy scarecrow.

The smell of beef and cabbage wafted from the tavern and made both their stomachs growl. Milán nudged his brother to bring his attention to the food scraps outside, then he was off, leaping across boxes and scooping as much food as he could into his threadbare shirt and running off. Jan followed suit. Within just two steps of making his escape, the boy heard the owner yelling.

"You filthy vermin! I'm going to chop off your fingers and feed them to my pigs!" He was fat but could move surprisingly quickly.

He chased the brothers down streets that stank of rotting food and human waste. They weaved their way between people, some who tried to grab them, others who yelled expletives at them as they were nudged out of their way. Dead animals lay in the street waiting to be swept into the river when the smell became too much. The brothers ducked into alleys and squeezed through cracks in fences. Milán turned and saw with despair that the fat tavern owner was gaining on them and had a spittle-flecked leer on his face at the prospect of impending violence. Jan grabbed Milán by the scruff of his neck and pulled him under some discarded rotten wood. The brothers peeked out from their fragile hiding place and saw the landlord wheeze and groan past. They waited a few moments then tentatively broke cover and walked in the opposite direction. When they were sure that the fat landlord was not going to swoop, the brothers looked at their booty and were so hungry that they had begun to salivate.

A half-eaten apple, some sprouting potatoes, two onions on the turn, and some peelings.

"He threatened to cut off our fingers for this?"

As distasteful as it was, they set about devouring it. They were so engaged in their food that they failed to see someone walk up behind them.

"Would you boys be interested in making some money?"

They looked up and there was a thin, gray man in a gray suit, with a half-smile on his face. Jan reached for anything he could find to defend himself and found a rotten branch.

The man laughed and held his hands up as though he was indulging a playful nephew.

"I assure you, there's no need for that. We're all friends here."

Jan dropped the branch, reached out, and squeezed his brother's hand.

"Make money doing what?" asked Milán.

"I don't trust him," Jan whispered.

"Very well." The gray man sighed and turned to walk away,

"Yes! Yes! We want to earn some money!"

At first the gray man had cut an impressive figure, but upon closer inspection Milán noticed that the handkerchief in his pocket was just a piece of cloth sewn in. The suit was frayed around the edges and had holes in it. His shoes were scuffed and dirty. He had a hungry, restless manner when he looked at the boys.

"We have no choice," Milán whispered to Jan.

As they followed the man into an unsure future, Jan tried

to pull away from his brother. He was on the verge of tears. Milán took his younger brother by the shoulders and looked him straight in his sky blues eyes, which sparkled in his muddy pudding face.

"I swear on our mother's grave that we will get out of here and the world shall know our voice."

CHAPTER ONE

The gargoyle is leering down at me. It's weathered and battered by New York pollution and weather but that does nothing to diminish its baleful glare or its power. I don't want to go in. Even from the grimy sidewalk and looking up I can feel the hotel throbbing with energy—an energy I haven't felt from the building before. It has more than its fair share of secrets and stories but usually it keeps them hidden behind the veil of a hotel that has seen better days. Something is happening behind those doors, something bad. I *really* don't want to go in, but I've had a cry for help. I shove my hands into the pockets of my hoodie because it's cold and because I'm looking for some antacids because just looking at that gargoyle is aggravating my reflux.

"I've never understood what a gargoyle is doing on a hotel. It doesn't exactly scream 'Come and have a restful time at the Cruthers Hotel!'" Clearly Marshall isn't as freaked out as I am.

I look across at him but he's already looking at his phone for a message that will never come. I look back at the Cruthers. The scaffolding around the frontage can't disguise its gnarly gothic overcoat, a barely contained snarling beast behind bars. Parts of it look more like a cathedral than a hotel, with its ornate arches, pointed buttresses, stained-glass windows, and the aforementioned gargoyle. It's said that, even though some of the rooms have floor-to-ceiling windows, light doesn't seem to be able to penetrate the gothic gloom.

"We should have better things to do than hang about a gone-to-seed hotel. We're two smart twenty-somethings. We should be doing—"

"Yeah?"

"Errr…" Marshall runs his hand through his curly black hair, and miraculously it springs back into its original shape. Maybe it's not so miraculous given all the time he spends on his appearance. Seems a little pointless to me, to be honest. He's wearing a shirt, which not only has a collar but which he also ironed. I mean, who even irons anything anymore? Well, Marshall, I suppose.

"You know the reason we're here."

"Hmmm? Yeah, good point well made," he says looking down at his phone. "Maybe I should ring her?" Marshall's frowning. "I mean, Kim might not even…"

I look at him, smile, and put my hand on his shoulder.

"I know," he says. "Sorry." And puts his phone away.

"What would you prefer to be doing?" I ask him.

"We could…" His face scrunches up as he thinks. A couple of seconds pass before he clears his throat. "Yeah, anyway, let's go and see what this emergency call from Spirits Unlimited is all about. They need rescuing again. You okay?"

"Yeah, I'm fine." But I'm not fine. I haven't been fine since we went to the Antarctic. At best I'm eighty-five percent. But I don't want to worry Marshall, so we enter the Cruthers Hotel and I instantly hear the babble of voices, plus the babble of Marv's voice.

"It's a disgrace!"

"Morning, Marv."

We've got the angry Marv today. You get any number of different Marvs depending on what day of the week it is. I absolutely prefer the bouncy energetic Roswell-fanboy Marv to this angry militant one. I guess you could call him a fan of Phantoms Inc. Probably the only one. I hope he's still on his meds. The manic gleam in his eyes would suggest not.

His bale of haystack hair sits on top of a brown-eyed, moon face hidden behind a pair of black-rimmed, Harry Potter glasses. He's shorter than both Marshall and me by a good couple of inches, and he carries a few extra pounds than us. Marv is clenching and unclenching his fists. All he's missing is the steam coming out of his ears. I try to reassure him.

"Marv, we all know that this isn't the first time the Cruthers has had a refurb." I make sure my voice is low and I speak slowly. In effect I have become a Marv whisperer.

The Cruthers is a hotel almost drowned by its own history, a cinder block tied to its foot. It was a high-end establishment at one point. The building dates from just before the dawn of the twentieth century and has had a few spruce-ups in the past, but these days you don't have to walk too far past the front desk to pick up the whiff of damp and mold. Which is a shame because the general style is art deco, with wood-paneled rooms and tiled fireplaces.

In one of the enclaves in the reception area is an oil painting of the brothers who lend the hotel their name and its reputation: the Cruthers. The older brother is sitting in an armchair with the younger standing by his side. Physically they look completely different. The sitting brother is slight and willowy, and the standing brother is thickset and has a scar zigzagging the left side of his face. Whoever painted the portrait might have exaggerated the scar: it's an unusual element to feature in a portrait, which would normally be flattering, and this one is anything but. They've moved the portrait around the hotel reception area. They clearly have a problem with portraits, though, the same thing happens with the one of Major Talbot, who built the hotel. I don't why they just don't put it in storage. The darkness makes their glowering more pronounced.

I've been in the hotel countless times and haven't really taken the time to appreciate just how unique the building is. It's sort of like an old but slightly creepy uncle you only ever hit up for a loan—trust me on this 'cause I have a slightly creepy uncle who serves that very purpose.

Marv is having a meltdown about the Cruthers refurb and

I'm having to talk him down. Although how and why I've suddenly attained the role of geek whisperer I don't know.

"Yeah, I know, I know. I just get so…you know…"

"I know."

It might not be so easy to calm down the dozen or so NecronomiCon regulars he's managed to assemble to look awkward in the hotel reception. Bless them, even their spatial awareness is off, 'cause when they aren't on their phones they keep bumping into each other like a bunch of nerdy kittens trying to find their feet. The staff don't seem particularly put out by them—or they're choosing to ignore them. Marv leans in.

"We've got an ally."

I look around, and at first I miss all five foot nothing of our ally and have to stop myself saying "I didn't see you down there!"

"This is Eugene!" says Marv, and Eugene gives us a cheery wave. Marv towers above him and Marv ain't exactly Andre the Giant. Eugene is dressed in oil-stained overalls with a tool belt slung low around his waist like he's going to reach for a six shooter. He's got mismatched David Bowie blue and green eyes, and a pale complexion that suggests he doesn't get out much. He puts his hand out to shake mine.

"Phantoms Inc.! I'm a *huge* fan!" Marv's got competition!

"You are?" I shake Eugene's hand and have to resist the urge to wipe my hand on my Levi's.

"Eugene is the handyman around the Cruthers," Marv explains.

"Well, more a gun for hire." He goes for a hammer on his belt, which he drops.

"Yeah, well." Marv coughs as Eugene scrabbles for his tool. "Eugene has agreed to help us."

"But I can't be *seen* to help you. If Mr. Atherton was to see me talking to you…" he whispers, having reholstered his hammer. For someone who can't be seen to be helping us, he's got a funny way of being clandestine. Eugene is just out-in-the-open talking to us; he's hardly Jason Bourne. Not that the receptionists seem to give a shit.

"And who the fuck is *Mr. Atherton* when he's at home?" I ask and know from the look on Eugene's face that, whoever he is, he's standing behind me.

"I'm William Atherton, and I'm the manager of this hotel. And *who are you*?"

He's got ginger hair and a scrubby ginger beard. Atherton looks at us the same way I imagine that he looks at something on the bottom of his shoe.

"They're Phantoms Inc.!" Eugene says, and Atherton laughs, the cheeky fuck.

I hand him a business card—more to get rid of one, 'cause I don't think he's gonna put any work our way. We've got *thousands* of business cards. We were trying to think of a name for our fledgling business one night and kept coming up against a brick wall. Marshall suggested we get stoned. I'd never tried weed. We had a great night—I remember a lot of giggling. *However,* when we woke up the next morning we found that we'd bought a load of business cards—who even uses them anymore?—and the domain name phantomsincorporated.com for two years, so we kinda got stuck with it. But it ain't so bad. I've got used to being part of Phantoms Inc.

"And what are you doing here distracting Eugene, *Phantoms Inc.*?" he says with a sniff. He keeps the card pinched between his thumb and forefinger, handling it like I've just handed him a turd.

"We were just asking him about the ambitious refurb plans," I reply.

"Yes, yes they are ambitious." His eyes narrow. "Why do you want to know?"

"Just interested, that's all. We've been coming to the Cruthers for years."

"Well,"—he sniffs— "we won't be wanting your custom in the next few years. The hotel is moving in an exciting new direction."

"But it won't be the Cruthers!" Marv blurts out.

"That's exactly what we want. We're going to drop the Cruthers name. Too many *regrettable* associations. We've shortlisted a few options. There's no room for this kind of *legacy* hotel in the business. No, what we're going for is a more bespoke, bijou experience for the more discerning New York visitor."

"What about NecronomiCon?" I think Marv's gonna cry. His bottom lip is practically wobbling.

NecronomiCon is a convention that has had its home at the

Cruthers Hotel since its inception. Dark, musty enclaves with dark, musty people. It began as an event for weirdos with an H.P. Lovecraft obsession and now it's just become an event for weirdos—lovely and interesting weirdos, but still weirdos. This hotel seems to attract them like a weirdo magnet. Marshall and I tend to hang about there a lot and I have worked on a lot of hangovers while at the convention. It's also been a good place to network and get intel over the years. I guess I will miss it if it has to move. It won't be quite the same at your average airport Radisson.

"Oh yes,"—Atherton positively drips with sarcasm—"Necronomi*Con*. Well, I don't think anyone will be too heartbroken about that particular collection of people having to find a new dungeon to hang out in. I'm sure there's an abandoned garage somewhere that will have them."

Marv looks like he's going to explode.

"You two"—Atherton waves a hand at me and Marshall—"conclude your business and let Eugene get on with his work tasks." And with another sniff he's off. The prick. I hope he slips and falls down a manhole.

"Who the fuck does he think he is?"

"Well, he's the new manager of the Cruthers Hotel," I remind Marshall.

"No shit, Sherlock."

"What I mean is that he's the manager of the Cruthers and he's obviously been tasked with pushing through this refurb and we're...well, we're not."

Would it be so bad if they did a refurb on this place? Maybe not. There's an occasional smell of boiled cabbage that wafts across the rooms—to be fair, that may come from the attendees of NecronomiCon—and there are corners of the hotel that are building up layers of grime and cobwebs. It has begun to look very scuffed in the last few years. Certainly, they should get rid of the spooky portrait of the Cruthers in the reception area.

"I'm sorry about Atherton," Eugene says. "The truth is there's been a lot of strange things going on…"

"There's always strange things going on. This is the Cruthers. Look at the strange people hanging about."

"I know, I know, but it's started to get *really* strange since they started the refurb."

"Don't tell me, the ghosts don't like the new wallpaper?"

"What kind of strange?" I try to steer away from Marshall's attempt at humor.

"Noises, feet going up stairs when there's no one there, shadows seen out of the corner of people's eyes, and workers being scratched and pushed by unseen forces."

"Is stuff being thrown around? Things appear to levitate and then are smashed?"

"Yes! How did you—"

"Sounds like pretty standard poltergeist activity to me." I stifle a yawn.

Eugene looks crestfallen, and I look over his shoulder—which is not hard to do. We're not actually here to help Marv out: we're here because of a distress call I picked up from one of our least favorite people.

*

I wasn't doing anything, and I wasn't looking for anything to happen, but that's when these things always do.

I was in our apartment, which also doubles as our office in downtown Brooklyn. We'd had a run of two well-paid gigs. Which is pretty good for us. Klaus was cool, anyway. For once, he wasn't chasing us for the rent. I don't think he'd *really* throw us out. Marshall fixed some of the arcade games in Donkey King—below our apartment—for him, and something always turns up. In fact, at that point I think Marshall was out talking to Klaus about something. I was pleased to have a bit of breathing time. (On the topic of breathing time, maybe I should finally hunt down what the mystery smell is in our apartment. We've been able to mask it with air fresheners when clients have been in, but I think it's getting beyond that point now. I did some laundry and that helped to take the edge off the odor, but it's undeniably still there and getting worse.)

We had some downtime, which I was using to rearrange some of my action figures. I'm mainly into *Star Trek: Next Gen* and a new Hero line has been brought out. It's mainly repackaged. When I can, I buy one to keep boxed and one to take out to display. I'm a sucker for shiny new packaging. I'd *just* got the Colonel Worf figure from *Star Trek VI: The Undiscovered Country*, where Michael Dorn plays the grandfather of his *Next Gen* character. I'd put him next to my *Deep Space Nine* Worf figure—and it looked like his grandfather was telling him off, which made me laugh—when I got a sharp stabbing headache and a crystal-clear image of something that looked like a melted chocolate castle, which was rapidly replaced by Joey Santiago shouting "Help me!".

Joey is part of a sorta splinter group from us—and, unfairly, much more successful than us. They'd stabbed us in the back on a big case we were working on together and worked against us recently. We were friends, once. It's a long story. I'd heard at the last NecronomiCon that not only was there a big refurb going on, but that Joey and Davey—aka Spirits Unlimited (stupid name)—had been called in to investigate something. Marshall was furious, but I was fine with it. I hadn't been happy the last few times we'd been to the Cruthers Hotel. With a building that old, with its eldritch history, there's always going to be lurching memories and people, but recently it's felt more than that. It felt like something was building up, that something was about to explode. To be honest I think I was a bit relieved. Maybe the refurb could clear the air and they could deal with whatever supernatural volcano was simmering underneath.

Joey's SOS lasted for a total of three seconds, but when it ended I found myself on the floor. And I'd broken my new Worf figure, goddamn it. It took me a few moments to get to my feet, and my legs were a bit wobbly. Joey was in trouble and, despite everything, we had to help her. We were the only people who could. And that's how we found ourselves back at the Cruthers Hotel.

*

"You don't understand"—Eugene is still in full flow—"this *activity* has been forcing workmen away. They refuse to work on one floor in particular."

"But that's a good thing, surely?" Marv points out. "We don't want the refurb to go ahead." He blinks rapidly. "I mean, the Cruthers is *fine* the way it is! Why do they always have to go changing everything?"

"They've got to do something. They've been losing money hand over fist for years. If the new owners can't make this a going concern and make this refurb work, they'll sell the building. It'll be turned into apartments and I'll be out of a job."

"I'm confused. I thought you were against the refurb, Eugene?" Marshall says.

Both Marv and Eugene shake their heads vigorously, sending dandruff flying.

"Nononono!" Marv says, just to hammer home the point. "We want a *sympathetic* refurb. Just think of all the history this place has! They could really exploit that."

"Yeah, but the history is part of the problem. Look." Eugene shows us some recent Tripadvisor reviews for the Cruthers. They don't make for good reading:

"…terrible atmosphere, I couldn't sleep for more than 30 minutes without getting woken up. I think they have a problem with the plumbing. One star…"

"…our room was deathly cold…the staff sent workmen round, but the temperature was still freezing and they couldn't or wouldn't move me to another room. Avoid. One star…"

You get the picture.

"Yes, well,"—Marv coughs—"there's gotta be a compromise. When they see what strong emotions this fuels in so many of us."

Well, maybe it fuels strong emotions in you, Marv. I look around at the awkward bunch of individuals gawking at their phones and checking their watches. I don't hold out much hope for Marv's noble crusade.

Eugene is right, something has stirred up activity here. I can hear a crossfire of voices, some loud, some quiet. I suspect that the quiet ones are older, being slowly erased by the dust of the passing years, but I'm not picking up the voices that brought us here. I'm not picking up the voices of Spirits Unlimited.

"So…Seen Joey and Davey around?" Marshall asks, as though he's read my mind. That's been happening more often recently.

"Oh yeah! Atherton's got Spirits Unlimited in to investigate the *activity.*"

I see Marshall flinch at the mention our rival organization and I feel an involuntary twitch around my lips.

"Oh, did he? I hadn't heard," Marshall lies.

"Really?" Marv blinks. "I thought everyone knew!" Eugene kicks him, which just elicits an "Ow! What?"

"Where are Davey and Joey now?"

"I think they were on floor six and a half, the last I heard."

We all whistle.

"Floor six and a half? Really?" I'm impressed. If it had been us—*and it should've been us*—I would have gradually worked myself up to floor six and a half. It's a *hidden* floor, which hadn't been included in the hotel's original building plans. Its existence became more widely known last Halloween, shortly after Marshall, Marv, and I discovered one of Nikola Tesla's lost abandoned laboratories on the floor. It's a long story, but it's fair to say that since its existence came to light it's gained somewhat of a reputation, to the extent that some YouTubers have been breaking in and making videos, which have been shocking but not in a good way: a few bangs and an 'orb' and that's your lot. I showed Marshall some of the videos for a laugh, and initially he did laugh but then I think he was upset that he hadn't thought of doing a video when we were there—the hits on our YouTube channel have been way down recently. When we did have access to the floor, we were too busy following up a lead that Marv had supplied to get all *social media* on it. There've been reports of high strangeness even before these recent occurrences. Dark events from the ages have soaked into the walls of the hotel over the years and from time to time those events have replayed themselves, but they seem to have increased of late, leading to the floor being out of bounds. Now it looks like we're heading back up to floor six and a half.

"Okay then." I see a moment of doubt flicker across Marshall's face. "Well then, that's where we need to be." I grimace and he shoots me a look.

"That's gonna be a bit tricky," Marv says. "They've closed it off. There's been restricted access since the *incident*."

There's been an *incident*?

"A recent incident?"

Now it's time for Eugene and Marv to exchange a look.

"Yeah, it's been pretty – uh – major." Marv mumbles at his sneakers.

I try to pick up what this *incident* might have been but I'm not getting anything.

"Can you help us to get up to floor six and a half?" Marshall asks Eugene.

"Oooh, I dunno…" He shuffles from foot to foot.

"Go on, you know you'd be doing us a solid."

Eugene wobbles his head from side to side as though he's knocking his thoughts into shape and then cracks a smile.

"Ah go on then! Anything for Phantoms Inc.!"

As if from nowhere, Atherton appears and literally nudges Eugene out of the way. He's obviously overheard what we've been talking about. For a moment he just looks between the two of us then, with a hint of a smile on his exfoliated face, he says, "No, Eugene, you go about your business. I think I'll take them on a tour of floor six and a half."

CHAPTER TWO

Conner

I turn to follow Atherton but catch sight of one of the paintings propped up against the wall. It's a portrait of a woman with long jet-black hair, brown eyes, and an hourglass figure, wearing a 1950s dress. There's an odd purple haze to the picture, and she looks like she's pleading with me. There's no mistaking who she is. I feel like I've been punched in the guts. I can't handle this. I close my eyes and look away.

The murder of the Dark Orchid is one of the most notorious cold cases in American history.

Nicknamed "the Orchid" at school after the rare flower that grew in her native Brazil, Mary-Jane Mountmore came from out West to New York to make it big as an actress. There's been a lot of conjecture as to why the Big Apple and not the City of Angels. One story is that she was offered an audition here by a big studio; a letter was uncovered a few years ago but there were claims that it was a fake. Who knows?

Rumors continue to float around about what she was up to during her short and tragic stay in New York. She certainly went to a few—unsuccessful—auditions. That's about the only *fact* that can be verified.

Her horribly mutilated body was found three blocks away from the Cruthers Hotel. Some theories suggest that it was in accordance with an occult ritual. Rumor and counter rumor have swirled around the case for years.

The last time she was seen alive was at the Cruthers Hotel, and—of course—she's supposed to haunt the building. Marshall has tried to get me to tap into any echoes, but I've never had any whispers before. So why now?

*

The journal of Mary-Jane Mountmore

New York. The first thing I did when I got off the Greyhound bus was to cough. The air here is so thick here you could spread it on your toast, but here I am in dirty, wonderful New York. It's so busy here you have to run to stay still—but the thrill of it all! The electricity! The streets sing with excited chatter. The skyscrapers speak of opportunities and adventure. I feel so free! Out of the constraints and shackles of home.

Akron, Ohio, is a nowhere town in a nowhere state with nowhere people. Everyone knows each other's business and it drives me mad! If you wet your panties at a kindergarten party when you're four people will remind you of it throughout high school.

I did, and they did.

I've felt so caged in Akron and now I feel like I can finally spread my wings and fly! I've known since I was six that I wanted more than just to grow up to be someone's wife or work in one of the factories. I had so much bubbling inside me it felt like I could explode! And now here I am.

Lordy lord it was quite the trek! All that time on the coach with that twitchy guy sitting across from me talking to himself.

I'll never know why my granddaddy didn't just stay in New York. It would have been so much more exciting to have come over from my native Brazil to live with him there. Why settle for Akron? No one ever speaks about it. I dunno what the big deal is, and he never really spoke about his time here. That ain't gonna be me. Just before I left, my grandaddy said that he left something behind in New York. He mentioned something about having a storage space down the bay area. Bless him, I don't know if he was a little confused. I might check it out if I have time. He would mention some things but would then clam up, almost as though he was catching himself.

On the bus here I kept re-reading the letter from Fairfax Pictures. They want me to attend a screen test with a view to going under contract. It's like a dream! Everyone knows each other's business but I want everyone to know my name and my face from Timbuktu to Tokyo! I'm going to be a star! And I know how I'm going to do it. I know the place to go, the place it all starts.

I've got the newspaper article I kept at home like a talisman, all the money saved up from waitressing and babysitting, and here I finally am. Not quite in the Cruthers Hotel, but close by.

They don't know what's gonna hit them.

*

Conner

Something is happening in the hotel. I've never known it so active. First the Dark Orchid, and now there are voices swirling around. I reach inwardly for my Captain America shield—Phantoms Inc. is a Marvel house—and outwardly I reach for my antacids. The shield is a psychological method that Marshall helped me to develop. Whenever the voices threaten to overwhelm me, I imagine that I'm holding the Cap's shield up, and the voices bounce off it. It's helpful. Usually the antacids knock back the reflux, although I'm convinced I have a stomach ulcer despite what my doctor said last time. Right here, right now, all the shield and antacids can do is to take the edge off my anxiety. Above the voices is something else: it's not really a human voice, it's more like the growl of an animal. It has the same deep gruffness as the voice I heard here last year, which said, "We know who you are."

"You okay?"

"Yeah, just got a headache. Too much coffee."

"I did warn you."

"I know, I never listen. That reminds me, I've got to make an appointment with my doctor…"

"Oh Christ, not this again! How many times do you need

to be told you don't have a stomach ulcer? It's almost as though you're willing yourself to get one."

I don't think Marshall's being entirely fair, I've suffered with this acid indigestion for the last eighteen months and it's not getting any better—and the prospect of floor six and a half does nothing to help. Just because they haven't found anything doesn't mean that there isn't anything there. Maybe I should get a second opinion.

"Come on, let's go." Marshall says, shaking me out of the contemplation of my medical woes.

CHAPTER THREE

Marshall

"What's this incident?"

"It's hardly an *incident*. Eugene is one for the melodrama. It's easier if I show you. It's a storm in a teacup, really." Atherton takes two steps at a time and we struggle to keep up.

The corridor we walk down seems to have had work done since we were last there. We don't need torches this time. Plaster dust covers the carpet, and the wood paneling has been torn away. In the enclaves there's part of a plaster foot, which is all that remains of the Greek statues which used to be there. There's some scaffolding set up and some tools have been left around. There's a copy of a newspaper that's been left, with a discarded half-eaten sandwich and a Starbucks cup of half-drunk coffee by its side. There's a green plastic gun-like machine at the foot of the scaffolding. I take a look at it but resist the urge to pick it up 'cause I'd just pretend it was a laser gun. There are footprints in the dust.

I haven't got as much invested in the Cruthers as Marv or Eugene have, but even I have to admit that seeing the vintage decor ripped away with such little regard is heartbreaking. I think I sorta thought that the Cruthers would always be here—and of course it still will be, kinda, but it won't be the same. It'll be some homogenized shiny hotel, as common as rats. I guess all the weirdos—and us—will have to find another place to hang around in.

"What do you know of floor six and a half?" Atherton asks.

"Oh, this and that, but we don't know what's happened recently. Only the stories, the rumors."

Of course, we know a lot more than that.

"Some of the rumors are true." Atherton is so earnest that I have to look down at my feet to try to stop myself laughing, but when I look back up the expression on Conner's face changes. He's picking something up.

"Could we take a look inside?" Conner asks.

If only we'd brought the Backpack of Doom with us. The Backpack of Doom aka the BPoD is…a backpack, which contains loads of useful stuff like the Egg Scrambler, a *not quite legit* purchase that scrambles most surveillance cameras, and various tools to get us into places. I didn't bring it 'cause I didn't think we'd need it.

While he's been talking I've taken out a credit card—which is constantly being declined so it might as well be of some use—and slid it between the lock and the door. To my surprise the door opens. I hear Atherton spluttering complaints as we enter.

The room is in darkness, but I can make out two gargoyles similar to the one we saw on the outside of the hotel, and in a dark enclave there's a painting. I must turn the torch on my phone to get a look. It's a square canvas with purple oil paint laid over it in thick slabs. I'm about to turn away when I notice a detail in the bottom right scratched into the paint is a tiny flower. It's got an odd shivering effect.

I don't know much about art, but I know what I like—and I don't like this.

"Shall we leave?" Conner suggests.

I nod my agreement. there's something not right about this room—it feels like the walls are closing in on me—but when we get back out into the corridor and turn the corner, I wish I'd stayed in the room. We walk into chaos.

*

Conner

It feels like I've got a pair of headphones on that I can't take off, and someone is turning the volume up. This floor is buzzing with activity, and I can't distinguish the signal from the noise; there's a faint echo that might be coming from Joey, which I can't make sense of. I don't know if she's still here or if she left. It's like seeing ripples in a pond after a stone's been thrown in. As a result I'm only half listening to what's being said in the "real" world. Why is Marshall giving me a concerned look? I barely notice our surroundings until we turn the corner.

It looks like a tornado has swept through the corridor. Pieces of broken furniture and broken shards of mirror and glass crunch under our feet. I can smell burned toast. Oh God, I hope I'm not having a stroke, although that would explain a lot. There's huge chunks missing out of the wall, like gaping wounds in the flesh of the hotel, exposing the bare bones underneath. I pop two ibuprofen into my mouth and dry swallow.

"What caused the damage?"

"Oh, some of it was the refurb but most of it…There were two workmen up here. The security camera caught some of what happened, but…" He points at a smashed camera hanging limply from the wall.

"What happened to the workmen?"

"No one's seen them since." Atherton waves his hand dismissively, but on the far wall are two blast shadows in the shape of people. They remind me of pictures of what was left of the victims of the Hiroshima bomb.

Marshall reaches out and touches the shadows, getting gray ash on his fingertips, which he quickly wipes off on his jeans.

I have a horrible sinking feeling.

"So where are Joey and Davey? Eugene said they were up here."

"Yes, they came up here around four hours ago.

"They're probably skulking around here somewhere." But Marshall doesn't seem sure. We walk on a bit further.

"Can anyone smell…?"

"Burned toast?"

"Thank God it's not just me. I thought I was having a stroke."

"No, I smelled it back there and it's getting stronger."

"What are you doing here? I told you that I would deal with this." Atherton is glowering at Eugene, who has seemingly just materialized from nowhere.

"I'm sorry, Mr. Atherton. I…they…er…" he splutters.

"Yes yes yes. Get down to the toilets on floor two: they're blocked, *again*."

He nods, and begins to amble off, when Atherton calls him back.

"Give me your radio. I left mine downstairs." Eugene meekly hands it over and walks off.

"I suppose you want to see *the window?*"

"The window? I certainly don't remember there being any windows up here, but that was before this refurb

started – and we had other things on our minds.

Without any explanation Atherton swans off down the corridor patting his pocket. We trot off after him and he stops in front of an ornate stained-glass window. Either side of it are a pair of rather tatty and faded red velvet curtains. The window looks incongruous here, but it wouldn't look out of place in a church—except no church I know would have a stained-glass window depicting such an odd collection of things. There's a lot of things wrong about this window, but one in particular leaps out at me.

"Why has someone built a window into an interior wall that looks out at nothing?"

"Well, precisely." Atherton looks annoyed, like I've asked the most obvious question in the world. "Why indeed. I'm afraid you'd need to ask the original owner of this hotel, one Major Lawrence Talbot. But he's long dead."

The window is round, made up of three circles. On the outer circle are six symbols that look like runes straight outta Middle Earth. These surround six stained-glass panels with odd pictures. There's a tree, then what could be brambles—they certainly have sharp points. The third shows some kind of forest, then there's what looks like a red stone. The fifth shows a cave with a red ring around the entrance, and finally—and perhaps the oddest—what could be a castle, but it looks like it's made out of chocolate and has begun to melt in the sun. In the center of the window is just a plain piece of red glass, which doesn't seem too quite fit. I make a mental note.

Even though the window doesn't look out at anything, the circular red glass at its center seems to *glow.* It's probably a trick of the light.

Atherton clears his throat.

"The window—as you see now—is one of the original features, but the red glass looks like a modern replacement. It *should* depict Baphomet, a type of satanic goat god with a pentangle in the middle of its head. "

Yeahyeahyeah, I know what a Baphomet is.

"How do you know so much about this?"

"I have an interest in such things; that's partly what

persuaded me into taking the job." And he does an annoying gesture waving his hand around in the air.

Atherton's radio crackles into life, he presses a button, and puts his ear to the speaker.

"Yes? Okay, fine." A look of annoyance on his face. "I've got to get back to reception."

We both nod. I don't really know what reaction he wants from us.

"Oh, you two aren't staying up here. You shouldn't be up here to begin with. Your friends will probably be back downstairs now. I only showed you the window to get you out of my hair. So now you can follow me." With that he strides off, and we have no other choice other than to follow him.

CHAPTER FOUR

Marshall

When we arrive back at reception all the insipid protesters have left, leaving Marv standing on his own looking lost in front of the huge signature marble staircase, which is one of the few features to have retained a sense of dignity in the hotel—but it still looks like it could do with a good scrub. The whole place looks more worn out than I remember, and it's only been a few months since I was here last.

When he sees us, he becomes bouncy Mario Marv.

"Did Joey and Davey come back down?" I ask.

"No. Didn't you find them up there?"

"The *incident* you mentioned wouldn't have anything to do with those blast shadows up there, would it? Atherton seemed pretty cagey about it all."

I knew that would play well with Marv; he loves to be first with the intel.

"Let me get Eugene; he can show you. He downloaded the security camera footage to his phone."

With the mood he's in, it doesn't take Marv long to fetch Eugene and persuade him to let us watch all eleven seconds of the video. It shows the corridor we've just seen and two workmen hacking plaster off the wall. Everything looks normal, then a chair shoots across the space and smashes against the wall.

"Holy shit!" we hear one of the workmen say.

"Yeah, but that could be…" I start.

A table begins to levitate.

"No, that is impressive."

At this point the workmen are covering their heads, which is lucky as a mirror cracks sending shards flying outward. A gust of wind seems to blow through the space unsettling the debris.

"What the fuck is that?" shouts one of the workmen. The camera view of the corridor goes sideways, then disappears into static.

"What's wrong with Conner?"

"Apart from…" I start, but then I turn around and Conner has collapsed against a pillar. The blood has drained from his face. I rush over and support him before he falls over. It can't be the video, surely? He's seen much worse than that.

"Something terrible…something terrible is about to happen…We've got to stop it."

He drags me even as I'm holding him up and we do an

undignified lurch out of the reception area. For someone who was at death's door a few seconds ago he can really move. We race through corridors and rooms I've never seen before, until we reach a weathered crimson door with ornate carvings around the edge.

Conner stops dead.

He hesitates to go inside, but eventually pushes it open.

Although it's midday, it's dark in here. Maybe the curtains are shut. But when my eyes adjust, I can see that they're drawn back but no light is getting in.

We look at each other, turn on the torches on our phones, and walk in.

We walk into carnage.

The light from our phones reflects off glassy eyes, a mouth frozen in a rictus scream, and skin splattered with blood. The horror makes me numb and I run the light down the corpse. Her body has been hacked and separated at the waist.

I can't believe what I'm seeing, but I can't look away. She's surrounded by a halo of blood, which is slowly spreading and soaking into the wooden floor.

Both Conner and I are frozen to the spot until we hear Eugene's voice behind us.

"Oh my god! What have you done?"

CHAPTER FIVE

This job never gets any easier and I wish I could say that nothing surprises me anymore, but that would be a lie. I'm looking across at one of the people of interest that we brought up at the Addams Family hotel aka The Hollywood aka the Cruthers Hotel, and I just can't read him. We picked him and his work colleague up at the most brutal murder scene I've seen in my fifteen-year career in the NYPD. He's either completely stunned, from another planet, *or* is a very cold fish.

"So tell me"—I look down at my notes— "Conner…" I know his name; it's just meant to put him off, but he doesn't seem phased. "You just got"—I check my notes again; this time I do need them— "*drawn* to the room?" I sit back in my chair and put my skeptical face on.

"Yes, I have an ability."

"You're a medium?"

"Not so much, but if it gives you a context, then fine. When I walk into the hotel my abilities seem to be maximized."

"Must be interesting."

"That's one word for it."

"This ability led you to the murder site?"

"You can check your records. I've helped the police before with cases."

"Yes, I've read up about you interfering with evidence at a crime scene."

"That's not what happened. Joey—"

"Ah yes…Joey Santiago of…Spirits Unlimited—awful name; sounds like an album by Yes. Joey is currently missing. I don't suppose you know anything about that do you?"

He moves in his chair and there's a twitch.

"No, I know nothing about where Joey is."

He's lying. "Well, they haven't been officially recorded as missing, but if they are I'll be knocking on your door again."

This time nothing.

"The murder scene." I lay out the pictures before Conner, which makes him flinch. "Her name was Angela Maron, a twenty-five-year-old actress. Did you know her?"

Conner shakes his head. So far we've not been able to make a connection to him or Marshall, so he might be telling the truth. Might.

There's something he's not telling me.

"Wait here for a minute." As if he's going to go anywhere else. I walk out of the interrogation room and meet up with another detective to check that Marshall's story tallies with Conner's. It does, so I don't have anything to hold him on.

"You're free to go." I look him straight in the eyes. "If you remember anything—*anything*—that you think would be of relevance you need to contact me immediately."

Four words into the sentence he's looking away, and then he leaves without saying a word. I have a feeling I'll be seeing him again. In the meantime, I have some questions of my own for the other member of Phantoms Inc., Marshall Thompson.

"Tell me what Phantoms Inc. do." I have to look down at my notes to stop myself laughing at the name. When I look back up I can see in his eyes and thin lips that he's noticed.

"But I thought—"

"I'd like to hear you explain it."

"Well, we are private detectives *really*, but my colleague has certain…er…unique abilities."

"Such as?"

"Well, he can…Well, what I mean is…he can see things from the past just by having contact with an item. That must be the strangest thing you've ever heard, right?"

"No, not really. It's not such a unique ability, though, is it?"

"What do you mean?"

"Your rivals, Spirits Unlimited,"— I have to stifle another laugh—"claim to be able to do something very similar."

"I don't know what they claim."

"But you don't deny that you're rivals?"

"You…I…what I mean…" he splutters, and I decide to

change tack while I've got him off guard.

"Do you know anything about the disappearance of Joey Santiago and Davey Lovering?"

"I know less than nothing. Conner was the one who got the SOS."

"An SOS? What do you mean?"

"Well, Conner sorta got a distress call from Joey." Marshall grimaces and curls a strand of his hair round a finger. "Conner would be the best person to speak to about that."

"I see," I say looking down at my papers, which have nothing to do with what he's just told me. "So that's what you were doing at the Cruthers? Looking for Ms. Santiago and Mr. Lovering?"

"Yes."

"That's very convenient."

"Not really."

"I have it on good authority that you *have* had a fairly bitter feud with Spirits Unlimited."

"Good authority, eh?"

I nod.

He says something that sounds like "*Faulkmeyer*" under his breath.

"Look, it's true that Spirits Unlimited and us had some history…"

"I heard that you'd called it a betrayal."

"You're a good listener."

"It goes with the job."

"Like I said, we had history. But we came to the Cruthers to help find them, not anything else. Look, are you going to charge me with anything?"

I could detain him for further questioning but there doesn't see much point. You don't get to pick and choose what cases you get—and I know this one is gonna be a gigantic pain in the ass—and yet…and yet…there's something more than a bit different about this one. After fifteen years in the saddle I reckon I have a good eye for which way things are going, and I've been right about eighty percent of the time. This one, however, I dunno: it's in that twenty percent. I'm torn between face-palming myself at all the paperwork this is gonna create and the interesting roads this might lead me down. This certainly ain't the usual breaking and entering or attempted murder cases I get across my desk.

"No, you're free to go, for now."

Unlike his colleague, Marshall doesn't seem in any hurry to leave. .

"I was just wondering what you were doing after work."

I laugh. Is this douchebag trying to pick me up?

"It's just that my cousin works in an Italian restaurant four blocks from here and he owes me a favor."

He *is* trying to pick me up! I've got to admire his guts and he isn't bad looking, but his cousin owes him a favor? *Come on,* and that's ignoring the fact that I've just interviewed him about the disappearance of two of his rivals.

"I don't think you appreciate how serious your situation is, Mr. Thompson."

He leans back in the chair and smiles.

"I know it's serious, but it's not that serious, really."

"Why not?"

"Oh, it's Spirits Unlimited. Joey and Davey. Davey especially can look after himself. They'll turn up; they always do. I wouldn't be surprised if they'd done this for publicity. That's the type of dick move that they'd pull."

"Right. Well, that might be the case, but for now I'll have to decline your kind offer as this is still an ongoing investigation. And you seem to be forgetting that I found you at the scene of a particularly gruesome murder."

He looks disappointed and gets up to leave, but before he walks through the door he says, "Let me know if you change your mind about the Italian."

He's got balls, I'll give him that.

*

Marshall

"Fuck! Fuuuuuuuuck! We're in so much shit!"

"No, no, we're fine. What happened when she interviewed you?"

"Er, I tried to pick her up."

"What?"

"I couldn't help myself! I could hear myself asking her out and I couldn't believe it."

"We'll be fine," says Conner. "We've got nothing to hide."

"Fine? Are you fucking kidding? We were found at the scene

of a murder plus Joey and Davey are missing and we're the prime candidates for their disappearance!"

Conner begins to chew his lip and I take some deep breaths. I waited until we were three blocks from the police station until I spoke.

"Right, right. Let's not panic."

"But that's exactly what you just did!"

Conner's got me there.

"Okay, let's not panic *again*. We've got to find out what happened to Joey and Davey."

"Would now be a good time to tell you that I picked up a whisper from the Dark Orchid while we were at the hotel?"

"What?"

"Just before we went up to look for Joey. The stuff from room 342 must have been moved down to the reception area for the refurb. She was pleading for help, too."

"Do you think there's a connection?"

Conner's face tells me all I need to know. "Then we shouldn't put off investigating her murder any longer!"

CHAPTER SIX

Marshall

Every few years a book comes out claiming to have found new evidence and to have solved the Dark Orchid case, only to be followed a few years later by another book making similar claims but contradicting the conclusions of the previous one. And on it goes, its own sick little cottage industry at the expense of a poor woman who was in the wrong place at the wrong time.

Conspiracy websites have sprung up dedicated up to the murder and the many, many theories surrounding it. There's even a conspiracy theory that the Dark Orchid wasn't actually killed where she was found but was murdered at the Cruthers. There's all kinds of nutzoid "proof" to support this, but no one has ever explained what anyone would have to gain from that.

Her journal has been the holy grail for years in this case, OccultDarkOrchid.com states categorically that the journal names and is the key that will unlock the mystery of her murder, although how they would know this is anyone's guess. Tantalizing fragments have emerged, which have only stoked the flames, but the actual journal has never been found. A couple of years ago copies of some pages reputed to be from her journal appeared online. Initially it was thought to be a hoax, but the handwriting matched up. An *actual* hoax did turn up around four years ago, and the gossip went around NecronomiCon that Faulkmeyer had something to do with it—I wouldn't put it past him, the sleaze; probably did it to try and smoke out the real journal—but he kept silent on it and the gossip burned itself out.

Faulkmeyer is our go-to guy for hard-to-get stuff and access. Recently he got hold of research papers from someone who worked with von Braun on the Apollo missions in the 1960s. We needed them for a client. It's a long story.

This is how we find ourselves, almost inevitably, outside Faulkmeyer's brownstone.

"Are you sure there's no other way?"

"The murder is so shrouded in rumors that we'll only get an answer if I can get hold of something connected with her, preferably her journal. And the only way we're going to do that is…"

"I don't think Faulkmeyer will have the lost journal."

"Why not?"

"'Cause if he did have it, he wouldn't stop going on about it."

"Well, he couldn't 'cause—"

"I know *that*. We wouldn't walk in and find him idly leafing through: 'Hello gentlemen! Look what I'm reading!' No, he'd be dropping really heavy hints at every opportunity."

"Perhaps. Still—"

"I didn't *actually* think he had the journal; I said *preferably* the journal. I can work with anything she would have had contact with. With Faulkmeyer's network, and especially his interest in the Dark Orchid murder, he'll be able to put me in front of something connected with her, and I go can go from there."

Balls. He's right.

So with a heavy heart I go to ring the doorbell, but my hand falls through open space. Faulkmeyer takes a step back and I'm looking at his smug face.

"Gentlemen, I've been expecting you."

Oh great, and he's got in with a classic Bond villain line. He's slicked his hair back to hide the fact that he's losing it. It's not working, but it does make him look less like he's the caretaker of an abandoned fairground in a *Scooby Doo* episode.

"Right…right…well, we were…expecting to come over." Jesus, even I'm not convinced.

"Well that's good to know. Come in."

I think I might be blushing.

Faulkmeyer's wearing one of his oriental waistcoats. No doubt he's got a highly intricate story about how he got it, when in actual fact he bought it in Chinatown. And—of course—he has a cup of Earl Grey on the go.

How the hell can he afford this place? I'll never know.

I heard down at NecronomiCon that he actually *owns* this brownstone—the whole of it—outright. I thought it must be a dead, rich relative he'd inherited it from, but the word on the street—well at NecronomiCon—is that he bought it with his own money. What did he do to get that kind of money? Conner's first guess was making meth, but he'd just re-watched *Breaking Bad* so that doesn't count. My guess is that he's got some incriminating footage of some rich douchebag; that's more his style, but I'm just pulling that guess outta my ass. Space equals money in Manhattan, and he's got the cash and—I have to admit—the taste to have space. As far as I'm aware he lives alone; there's no—God help us—Mrs. Faulkmeyer. It doesn't seem right that he's got all this space to himself and I'm constantly tripping over Worf action figures and old copies of Marvel's *Tomb of Dracula* in our cramped office/apartment.

This place smells good as well; that's one of the other big differences. No hunting round here, checking if something has crawled into a corner and died. Today his office smells of cinnamon; the last time we were here, of lavender. I don't know how he does it. Faulkmeyer hasn't skimped on the interior decoration, either. The rooms we've seen—which is pretty much just the hallway and his office/parlor—have got a rich but tasteful look to them: polished wooden floorboards with thick rugs and heavy looking curtains. He does have the odd—and I do mean *odd*—item dotted about the place on display. There's a purple velvet scabbard on a black metal stand; the handle of the weapon it houses shines gold, and I bet it's ya actual real gold.

It's far removed from the mass-produced "collectibles" which litter our place.

His office is lined with bookshelves where he displays his first editions. I once made the mistake of taking a signed copy of *Dune* from the shelf while he was in the toilet—he's actually said no to me using the toilet, the prick—and I thought about slipping it into my bag, but I knew he'd miss it. I put it back right when I found it in plenty of time, but as soon as he came back he pointed to the book and said, with a face like thunder and a tremulous voice, "Who moved that?" When I fessed up he went into a droning lecture about how expensive it was and how a book of that age should only be handled with a special kind of glove, for God's sake. I tried my hardest not to look bored but, if anything, he looked angrier at the end of it.

I notice out of the corner of my eye that he's acquired a new edition of Lovecraft's *At the Mountains of Madness*. I say "new"; it's new to his collection. He wouldn't have it on his shelve for all to see if it wasn't a first edition and he didn't want to show off, the idiot. Waves of superiority waft off him along with whatever cologne he uses—and, let's make no mistake about this, it is cologne not aftershave. He does seem to have used too much; it's like he's been bathing in it.

"You seem to have got yourself into quite a mess at the Cruthers."

"It wasn't our fault!" Conner blurts out.

"How do you know about that?"

Faulkmeyer waves his right hand around in the air as

though he's trying to conjure a portal to another world. "Word gets around. I don't know how I can help you, though. If it's an alibi you're after, I'm afraid—"

"The Dark Orchid!" Conner blurts out again.

Faulkmeyer leans back in his chair and narrows his eyes. "What about her?"

"Her murder is tied up with this. I need a way to get a connection to her. Maybe her journal?"

"That hasn't been seen in decades."

"It doesn't have to be the journal; it could be anything."

"No can do, I'm afraid. I've never been able to come by anything related to the tragic Mary-Jane. And believe me, I've tried."

"Shit."

We look at each other. I don't know what we can do. Our usual fallback for this eventuality would be to knock about the NecronomiCon at the Cruthers, but even if the refurb wasn't underway there wouldn't be one on the cards for a few months.

Faulkmeyer leans forward. "I can, however, go one better than any*thing*."

Prick. I don't know if I want to punch him in the throat or give him a hug.

"I can put you in touch with her agent."

"He's still alive?"

"Yes, he's still alive, and Francis owes me a favor."

Francis! Get him.

"Although I will warn you: all I can do is to provide an

introduction; he's notoriously private and grumpy."

He sounds like a riot. I have read that, in some eyes, he's the prime suspect in the murder of his most famous client.

"He hasn't spoken on record to anyone about the Dark Orchid for fifty years, but I'll get your sneakers in his door." Faulkmeyer looks pleased with himself.

"What do you want in return?"

The prick has the brass balls to look offended.

"You're going to do this out of the kindness of your heart?"

"No need for sarcasm, Marshall. What I was going to say is that, if this does go anywhere, I get a cut of any profits."

"Any profits?" Now Conner seems insulted. "We're fighting for our freedom!"

"No need to be melodramatic. I'm sure that Marshall has given thought to the financial benefits of finally solving the Dark Orchid murder."

I had, actually. "That's appalling, even for you! How much were you thinking?"

"Marshall!"

"Twenty percent from any media or merch."

"Ten percent."

"Fifteen."

"It's a deal. Do you want me to sign anything?"

"No need, I taped our entire conversation."

"Of course you did."

*

Have you seen Durham?

An eager-looking collie, tongue out, looks out from a poster taped to a telephone pole. There's only one telephone number slip to be pulled off, so Durham seems to have been missing for a while. Poor Durham.

"I can't believe you made that deal with Faulkmeyer. We're talking about someone's murder!" Conner is still sulking.

"It got us this lead, didn't it? We haven't got anything else to go on."

He mutters something under his breath but still follows me to the condo. We're on the outskirts of the city and, apart from missing dogs, it seems like quite a sleepy suburb.

We find ourselves outside 435 The Pines. The condo has seen better days. I think the exterior was painted white maybe a decade or two ago, but it's a sorta curdled creamy color now, which has started to peel. There are a few roof tiles missing, which is fine because there's a fair amount of moss growing to cover most of the holes. One of the gutters is trying to break away and is just hanging on by a screw, a wing, and a prayer. Water is leaking down from the gutter into a large blue barrel, which is overflowing onto the sodden ground.

One of the grimy windows is being held together with sticky tape. The only things that mark the condo out as not being completely abandoned are that there are lights on— which could actually mean it's a crack house—and, randomly, the front door looks very new, as though it's been changed in the last few months. The area immediately surrounding the front door is very well maintained, with no weeds or junk mail.

There are two flourishing flowerpots either side of the door. It might even have been freshly swept. Perhaps Francis Gold is still trying to fight the good fight against entropy and this is his last stand?

I head up to the sparkly door and ring the bell. I let a few seconds go by and then knock the door, then leave some more time pass before I check the address that Faulkmeyer gave us. I'm about to give up when I hear some movement, a shuffling sound coming from the other side of the door. A series of bolts is unlocked and, with some grunts, the door is opened by an elderly stooped man. His white hair is plastered over his head and his rheumy eyes look up at me.

"Mr. Gold? We've been sent by…"

He nods, rolls his eyes, and makes a gesture with his hand to follow him back into the condo. We walk into his living room, which is heated to the temperature of a reptile house. The condo smells of mothballs and its walls are chock-full of framed playbills, reviews, and movie posters. Randomly there's a huge, framed oil painting of Dolly Parton over the chimney breast. I can't see any mention of the Dark Orchid. The decor has been yellowed by the combination of years and nicotine. In the center of the room is a pock-marked mahogany table with a collection of mugs, an overflowing ashtray, and some new posters asking if anyone had seen Durham the dog. Ah! So…

"Thanks for seeing us, Mr. Gold."

He's already sat down and begun to smoke a future addition

to the ashtray. I notice that, among the detritus on the table, is—I presume—Durham's dog collar. Some of the mugs have cigarette butts floating in them, just to mix it up.

"Goldstein," he says and follows it with a phlegmy cough.

"What?"

"Call me Mr. Goldstein. I shortened my name in the fifties for…professional reasons."

"Right, well thanks for seeing us, Mr. Goldstein."

He gestures for us to sit down.

We wait for him to talk, but he just gazes down at the picture of his dog and smokes.

"Um, Faulkmeyer said…"

"I know what Faulkmeyer said," snaps Goldstein. "I can't help you."

"But Faulkmeyer—"

"I told Faulkmeyer I'd meet you, and that's what I've done. That slimy son of a bitch can consider his favor paid back in full."

Conner reaches out for something on the table.

"Please, we really need your help."

"I don't see how I can help you."

"We just need something related to The Dark Orchid…"

"Get out!"

Oh shit, this ain't going well.

Goldstein stands bolt upright and the years seem to fall away in his fury.

"I'm sorry, Mr. Goldstein, I didn't mean to—"

"Get the fuck out of my house!" he screams. And now comes the pushing. He's a lot stronger than he looks.

"I know where your dog is."

We both stop in our tracks and look at Conner. He's holding the dog collar.

*

Conner

I could see the situation going south. Usually I can't pick anything up from pets, apart from fleas, but since our last visit to the Cruthers my abilities seem to have shifted up a gear. As soon as I walked into the condo I was getting echoes, forlorn whispers from the ages, soon to be silenced forever. But the strongest echo I was getting was from the threadbare dog collar. I picked it up and could instantly see what had happened.

"I can take you to Durham. He's hungry, he's scared, but he's alive. We'll need a shovel."

Twenty minutes later—Goldstein isn't quick on his feet—we're on some shrubland near a forest and see rabbits running around. I lead Goldstein and Marshall to a fox hole and point.

Goldstein looks between the two of us, puts his hand on the small of his back, and kneels down with a groan before calling

"Durham? Durham?"

From the depths of the hole comes a faint whimper.

"Durham! Durham!" For the first time since we met Goldstein his face cracks into a smile.

Marshall uses the shovel we've brought to dig out some of

the hole and Durham is able to scrabble out. He's painfully thin, wet, but instantly licks Goldstein's face when he sees him.

"Thank you for finding my mutt."

*

The mutt in question is currently in the corner wolfing down some steak, which I can see Marshall eyeing with envy.

"He's the only thing with a heartbeat that I've given a shit about in the last forty years." Goldstein looks across at a framed photo of two very dapper gentlemen in dinner suits, standing close together, glasses of champagne in their hands, and I realize that one of them is him.

He snaps out from his reverie with a heavy sigh. Since he came back he's gone and found a thick sweater, which is unbelievable as the thermostat in this place must be screaming. He must pick up on my incredulity. "The cold gets right into the marrow of your bones, especially this time of the year."

It's spring.

"It'll happen to you." He wags a boney finger in our direction before adding, "If you're lucky."

"So, yeah – uh - the Dark Orchid?"

"Okay, okay. But don't call her that. I hate it. It just reduces her. It's disrespectful."

"Sorry. We're looking into the murder," Marshall says.

Goldstein nods and raises his eyebrows as though he's heard it all before.

"Genuinely, I don't know if there's anything I can tell you that I haven't said before, and it's been many many years."

I can almost see the regret and years pushing his shoulders down.

"I was her agent and I should have looked out for her," Goldstein says with a deep sigh. "I should have been a friend to her. This business eats its young, shits them out, and then slouches onto the next meal." Another heavy sigh. "I dunno what I can tell you fellas." He looks very tired.

Goldstein utters a groan as he gets up from his chair and removes the cushion that has stuck to his back. The crack as he stands makes me and Marshall wince. He hobbles over to what looks like a shoe box on the mantelpiece and brings out a red leather-bound book with a faded purple ribbon. Reverentially he hands it to Marshall.

"One thing I need to say to you fellas: beware the Infidels. Delicately Marshall opens it up and starts to read.

CHAPTER SEVEN

Marshall

We're both giggling as soon as we've turned the corner from Goldstein's condo.

"Why didn't you tell me that you could find lost dogs? We could do *that* for a living! Balls to being spirit sleuths!"

"I don't know how I did that." Conner rubs the back of his neck. "I seem to be able to do more. I could sorta hear Durham barking when I looked at the collar. I didn't even have to pick it up and handle it. I'm just glad we got the dog back. He seems like a lovely dog and Mr. Goldstein seemed pleased."

"No shit." I laugh. "Have you been able to pick anything up from the journal yet?"

Conner runs his palm across the cover with a pained expression on his face. I don't know what that means. It might mean he's got gas or is obsessing about his phantom stomach ulcer again.

"Nah, I'm getting nothing."

"You could find a lost dog using a dog collar but nothing from this?"

He shrugs. "I dunno. It comes and goes."

"Don't worry. We've got time." I laugh again and take the journal back off him. "Do you know what this means?"

"Yes, yes. He did say we could keep it, didn't he?" asks Conner.

"Yep, and we've got his signed authority saying as much. Fuck, he must really love that dog. I want to go up to Faulkmeyer and say, 'How do like those apples!'…Are you picking anything up now?"

"No, but that warning about the Infidels? What was that about? We're going to have to do some digging…"

Right on queue Faulkmeyer rings.

"How did it go with Francis, that old huckster?"

Does he know already? He's not usually this cheery with me.

"Goldstein? Oh yeah, it went…okay."

"Did you get much out of him? He can be a bit of a slippery character."

"Oh, you know, this and that. We helped him find his dog."

"His dog? Why…? Never mind…Sooooo, he *was* helpful?"

"Yeah, a bit." It's great to be the one who can be cagey for a change. Man, I can almost hear Faulkmeyer sweating. I'd love to know why Goldstein owed him a favor. "Actually, there's something you can help us out with."

"Anything." He definitely knows *something* about the journal.

"What do you know about the Infidels?"

For a while there's silence at the end of the line. "Why do you need to know about the Infidels?"

*

We find ourselves in an unusual situation. We're in Faulkmeyer's web of fear. but we're the ones in control(Ish).

"We just need to know anything you know about them."

Faulkmeyer rubs his chin. "The Infidels were an exclusive club, or a black magic coven, depending on which story you believe. The truth is probably somewhere in between. They met at the Cruthers from the time when the brothers ruled the hotel. In one telling of the story it was actually the brothers who set up the Infidels. Ostensibly it was just an excuse for some socialites to indulge in some swinging courtesy of Crowley's sex magick."

Conner and I look at each other. "Who wouldn't?" I say with a shrug.

Faulkmeyer's eyes narrow. He smiles and looks over at his bookshelves. "I'm surprised that you are asking about them because they are supposed to have gone to ground when the brothers disappeared."

"So why would Goldstein have mentioned them in connection with the Dark Orchid murder?"

"Yes, file them next to the Knights Templar, they're one of those groups who are meant to be behind everything and pulling the strings in every unexplained event. The difference with the Infidels might be that they actually *did* pull some strings. If they've resurfaced and are involved, you'd better watch your step. You'd need to find out who the new coven leader is. That would be your best bet for defeating them: cut off the head."

I don't know about cutting heads off. I'm a lover not a fighter. "What's so terrible about the Infidels? Isn't it just a posh boys' club?"

Faulkmeyer leans back in his chair, shakes his head, and sucks air through his teeth. "Bad people doing bad things. You've been up to floor six and a half; did you see the room where it happened?"

His head tilt and long pause suckers me into thinking that he actually wants to hear my reply, but I should have known better.

"The story goes that the body of a man was found with half his face missing. Some say that he offended Milán—the older brother and de facto leader of the Infidels—but the other theory is that he was sacrificed as part of some arcane occult ritual, and that now his ghost haunts the corridors of the hotel."

"What the fuck?" I say, glad to get a word in. "The Infidels got grabbed for that?"

"Ah, no. The Infidels were nowhere to be seen, and they all had alibis for that night. They got off scot-free."

I shake my head. "Who was the man they found?"

"That's the thing: they never identified him. All the labels had been cut out of his clothes and he had no ID on him. No one came forward to claim the body." He leaves a long pause, but I refuse to fall for it again. "It's one of the unsolved mysteries that float around the hotel."

"But I'm sure you have an opinion…" I know he will; he loves gossip.

"The lead theory is that he was a businessman from Utah."

"Ah the most sinister of states!"

"Indeed!" He misses my sarcasm, but I get a smirk from Conner.

"The mystery man had an interest in the occult, which led him to the Cruthers and to the Infidels. Hence the ritual theory. However, the brothers are also said to have dealt with dissension in the ranks in a similarly ruthless fashion. But that backfired on them big time: it caused a rival group, the Mescaleros. The *original* Mescaleros were a nomadic mountain people. Of course, it doesn't explain why the splinter group adopted their name. It's been suggested that their leader perhaps had Mescalero ancestry. The Infidels thought they'd wipe them out, but the grew in strength. They fought a blood-drenched secret war for supremacy in 1914 for supremacy and, in particular, to own the legendary Baphomet centerpiece."

Conner.

"It is the stuff of myth, but people were willing to go to war over it. And, as is often the way when war is waged, bystanders got hurt and killed. Have you ever heard of the Rivers Avenue massacre?"

"Yeah, I thought that had something to do with the mafia?" I say.

Faulkmeyer shakes his head. "No, it was a bungled attempt by the Mescaleros to ambush the Infidels. They hacked down whoever they found, but the Cruthers and some acolytes managed to escape. Twenty people died that night. Most had nothing to do with the feud between the Infidels and the Mescaleros."

"They slaughtered innocent bystanders?"

"I wouldn't say innocent, by any means. There were members of the mob there that night. The Infidels weren't averse to doing business with the underworld in every sense of the word. That's probably where the rumor that it was a mob hit came from, and the Mescaleros weren't averse to retaliating with the same type of violence.

*

"What do you make of that back there? What Faulkmeyer said? Why do we keep hearing about the Infidels?"

"Dunno." Conner shrugs, but I think he knows more than he's letting on.

I don't think any of us got what we really wanted from that meeting. It's then that I remember something I needed to talk to Conner about.

"Have you rung your mom back yet?"

"Uh? Conner suddenly finds something really interesting to look at on the sidewalk.

"Your mom? She rang and left a message with me, remember?"

"Oh yeah." He's rubbing the corner of his eye. "I'm gonna ring her back. It's just, you know, just haven't had the time." He runs his fingers through his blond thatch of hair, which, despite his best efforts, resists all attempts to be tamed into a reasonable style.

"What do you mean you haven't had time? You rearranged your action figures *again* last week!"

"I know, I know," he says as we both sidestep an irritating little dog which is being given too much lead by its owner, who is happily chatting on her phone while their mutt barks at us.

"It's just—"

"Listen. Ring your mom back. Just leaving it is only making it worse. It could mean we could get out of Donkey King."

Conner looks hurt.

"There's nothing wrong with Donkey King."

"I'm not saying there's anything wrong with Donkey King. It's just"—I give him a playful kick with my sneaker which elicits an equally playful—I hope— "Ow!" from him—"it's just we need to get out of there before your action figures kill us." This gets a laugh from him. "We're only one Riker variant away from them all coming down, crushing us!" We both laugh.

A cyclist on the pavement narrowly misses Conner. I give him a hard stare, which obviously does no good because he zooms off. I just hope a cop picks him up down the line.

"Anyway, yes"—I continue— "it would just be nice to have some space, wouldn't it?"

He nods.

"And we still haven't managed to get rid of that smell in the apartment. When we found that bag of moldy oranges behind the couch I thought we had it, but if anything the smell's gotten worse since we put it in the trash!"

"I will ring my mom back, but there's no guarantee that she'll be able to help us out."

I put my hands up in a gesture of surrender/acknowledgment and nearly hit a passerby in the face. "Sorry!"

But he gives me the evil eye.

"But equally she *might* be able to help us out. She's certainly been trying to build bridges in the last few months."

"No, I will ring her," he says. "It's just…you know…"

"Yeah, I know. She's hard work." What I leave unsaid is that she isn't as hard work as my dad, but I hope that's a bridge we won't have to cross.

At least I've got that out in the air. It's been going around in my head for days, so we're on the upswing.

I'm wrong. Things are about to get a lot worse.

Detective Murray is waiting for us and she's looking grim.

Marshall Thompson, Conner Deal, you're under arrest for the murder of Francis Goldstein. You have the right to remain silent. Anything you say can and will be used against you in a court of law…"

CHAPTER EIGHT

The journal of Mary-Jane Mountmore

Goldstein has put me up for auditions. Just bits and pieces: waitresses, receptionists, that type of role. So here's the thing: what's the difference between leaving your job as a waitress and actually *pretending* to be a waitress and having one line—if you're lucky—saying, "Ya want more coffee, hun?" I guess the difference is ten bucks, a lot of hanging about, and you don't have to go back and do it again the next day. That's got to be a good thing?

Every audition I go for I think it's going to happen and I'll finally get my foot in the door, finally. Taking the subway to some crummy studio somewhere while I try not to notice the casting director looking down my top. Then I hear that they've decided to use someone else.

Desperate times, desperate times. I've been going to the Cruthers in an effort to see and be seen. I've got Henry, my bartending friend who'll let me drink for free cause he says he's "a sucker for my lucky, pretty eyes". Corny, but I like him. And it's either accept his come-ons and drinks or make a club soda last all night.

I've met some people but I'm not sure what to make of them. There was a group of them in the bar last night. They had chosen a dark corner where light fears to tread. There were four of them, all men. They were watching the people in the bar in an amused, detached manner, as though they were looking at animals in a zoo. The most striking was a tall, thin man with swept-back peroxide blond hair and cheekbones you could slice bread with. I felt a magnetic pull toward him. He smiled as I approached him, as though he was expecting it.

Men usually make the first move. I hung about on the edge of the group looking disinterested but the blond man didn't bite. I sidled a little closer and waited for a break in the conversation.

"I haven't seen you around here before." I could grind my teeth at how awful my line was, but he just smiled at me.

I'm surprised I got further than my opening line, it was so bad, but he seemed to know that I was an actress and said that he had contacts. I can normally pick up something about people, what their angle is, but I was getting nothing from this one. He was guarded, only saying that he was in the movie business "in a manner of speaking". I expected the dangle of an "I can help your career" come-on, but it never came. What he said —and this I remember because I was worried he might be an evangelist—was "Have you ever thought there might be more to life than this? There are people you need to know, knowledge that you must learn, and worlds you must see if you are to achieve any of your dreams and beyond."

I nodded and smiled but I only understood half of what he was saying. So I decided to hit him with the old eyes down, back up, chest out, sweep hair back, and introduce myself, which always knocks 'em off their feet.

"My name is Mary-Jane Mountmore. My friends call me May."

"I know," is all I got from him, and that amused smile. "My name is Miles Hamer, and we are the Infidels."

CHAPTER NINE

Marshall

"What are you two doing back here?" Atherton sniffs. "I thought you'd been arrested. Best place for you."

Detective Murray doesn't have any evidence on us cause there a none to be had, maybe she was thinking of taking me up on my offer? I wouldn't be surprised, I thought we had some chemistry. Course Atherton doesn't need to know any of this, so I answer a question with a question.

"How did you know about that?" I ask, but Atherton only twirls his hand in the air, as though that's supposed to answer our question. He turns sharply and points at us.

"I heard something about…a journal?"

"Journal? What journal? We don't have a journal! Dark Orchid? I don't know what you mean!" Conner blurts out. Jesus. He'd make a terrible poker player.

"I never mentioned the Dark Orchid." Atherton leaves with

that hanging in the air like the Cheshire cat's smile.

I punch Conner in the shoulder.

"Ow! That's my bad shoulder!"

"Why did you say that whole thing about the Dark Orchid, you dingus?"

"Sorry, I got nervous."

"No shit, Sherlock."

Eugene pokes his head round a pillar.

"Has Atherton gone?" he asks. "I know he's my boss but he sorta gives me the creeps. I thought this is the last place you'd want to be, after, you know…"

"Yeah, well, someone or *something* is gunning for us. And we've gotta find out where Joey and Davey are."

"Do you want to go back to floor six and a half?" He leans in and I get a small whiff of cheese puffs. "The weirdness? It's gotten worse."

"Then we've gotta get back up there! We've got to find out what's happening."

I'm not sure there's any need for all this clandestine nonsense. Atherton is a bit slimy, but I wouldn't say he's creepy, not compared to some of the characters who hang out at the Cruthers. Anyway, I think Eugene brings more attention to us by scuttling around the place. I think he's doing his own particular style of cosplay. He's an odd guy, even in a room of very odd guys. He doesn't look like he quite fits into his skin. Eugene is all elbows and knees; it's like he's got an extra shin or something, which shouldn't be there. He's all right angles and awkwardness. I've seen Eugene when he thinks no one is looking and he's observing people: his eyes are narrowed and his lips are moving silently, speaking to himself, and I can see his thumb twitching. It's like he's processing something. I realize that he's actually just trying to fit in; he's looking at what everyone else is doing and trying to copy it. I have more than a little sympathy for what he's trying to do.

I fall back and hide myself behind a pillar so I can check my phone. I don't want Conner to see me 'cause he'll only give me *that look.* There's no messages.

"Have you been checking your phone again?"

"Fuck! Don't sneak up on me like that, Conner!"

"I didn't sneak up on you."

He did. "I'm not *checking* my phone…"

"She won't text you just 'cause you're checking your phone."

"I don't know what you're talking about. Anyway, as I said, I wasn't checking my phone, I was"—I've had time to think of an excuse—"I was…"

"Yes?"

"I was, uh, just checking out some new music, adding it to my playlist."

"Not Taylor Swift *again*?"

"Hey, don't be hating on TayderTot! Anyway, it's not Taylor Swift, it's Ariana Grande."

"She's just as bad!" He snorts and we both laugh, but I mean…he's got six different—I've counted them—Captain

Picard action figures and he's got the brass balls to criticize my taste in music?

"You know I'm right about checking your phone, though, don't you?"

I do. It's really annoying when he's right; good that it doesn't happen often. I decide to change the subject, then notice that Conner looks like he's been hit on the head with a brick.

"How are you feeling?"

"Yeah, good. You?"

"You okay to go back to floor six and a half?"

"Yeah, fine. Fine." He starts to chew his bottom lip.

"You're not fine, though, are you?"

"I've had another message from Joey. We've got to find the Baphomet centerpiece. And she said that time is running out!"

"Atherton seemed to know a lot about it. Perhaps we could ask him."

"I don't trust him. And Eugene's just the handyman. But…"

I know where this is going, and I don't like it.

*

Conner

We're back at Faulkmeyer's brownstone and it's clear that he'd been holding back on us the last time. We're sat in front of his desk, he's got a fresh Earl Grey on the go, he tents his fingers, and begins.

"One of the pioneers of the Infidels' occult practices was Major Lawrence Talbot, an adventurer of the other world, who—I'm sure you know—built the hotel. A colorful character even by the standards of the Cruthers. He was alleged to have left England because of a terrible family scandal, but historians have never been able to find any evidence of this. Even his title has been called into doubt. Much the same way as Elvis' manager 'Colonel' Tom Parker gave himself his rank, the same may have been the case for the Major."

"He was into all that other world stuff already? So did he find it there, or did it follow him?" Marshall asks.

"He picked the location very deliberately. There are places in our world that act as crossroads. Where the wall between our world and other realms is thin and, given the right knowledge and rituals, can actually be breached. Talbot built the hotel to a very specific and esoteric plan to build a bridge to traverse the hidden realms.

"Many had tried over the years—and some had even succeeded—to get to the realm of World Ash, or Yggdrasil. Those very few who had managed to get back were reluctant to reveal what they had discovered. All that was written down was that it was a forest realm and that within the forest lay great power, which could be harnessed by those with the right arcane knowledge. There were even those who whispered that World Ash held the secret to immortality, that a person who lived within the realm could live forever. Talbot hungered for the knowledge and that power."

"Fruit loop." Marshall snorts, but that doesn't put Faulkmeyer off his stride; he just takes a sip of his Earl Grey.

"Regrettably, Lawrence Talbot died in mysterious circumstances before he could really road test what he'd built, but he paved the way for others to follow him, namely the Cruthers brothers. Milán scoured the occult bookshops of the US buying anything he could about World Ash.

"All his research led to one further name: Nestor. At first it wasn't certain that this Nestor was even still alive. Nestor was part Cherokee and had some connection to a well-known and wealthy banking family in Manhattan. He had traveled the world in search of experience and occult knowledge and upon his return to Manhattan had helped Talbot design what was then the Grand Hotel. After Talbot died Nestor went on walkabout and whispers of encounters and appearances filtered down the years and eventually landed at the feet of Milán. It's not recorded what Milán did next."

Thanks, and all, but we could have got that online, or from Marv. How does that help us? Someone seems to want to frame us for two murders and the disappearance of Joey and Davey. And what about Dark Or— ""I assume you've seen the window." Faulkmeyer tilts his head in the way that I know is calculated to annoy Marshall and leans back in his chair.

When he seems lost in his thoughts I cough and Marshall says, "Atherton mentioned something about a missing centerpiece?"

"Atherton seems to know a lot about the window. Yes, the Baphomet centerpiece is what's supposed to marry the elements of the window together. The rest of the panels provide a one-way trip to the realm but the central panel provides the way back to our world. The panel was created in the 1850s by an Egyptian artisan called Amenhotep. It was reported that he had been passed arcane knowledge from his forefathers, which went back to the time of the pharaohs. It isn't known who Amenhotep created the central panel for, but he disappeared shortly after he'd completed work, as did his creation. But it is said that if you looked closely at the panel you would see into an evil realm beyond our world. Legend also has it that if you looked too long you would lose your mind." He undermines the gravitas by giving a little chuckle.

"It's lost or destroyed?" I ask. "And, if it's not too much trouble, *still* how does this hel—?""It was said to have been in the cargo hold of the Titanic when it set sail"—Faulkmeyer continues, seemingly oblivious to, or simply enjoying Marshall's growing impatience—"which doesn't really explain how it eventually resurfaced in New York."

Legend has the central panel appearing at key moments over the coming decades, usually associated with tragedy and death. Woven into its history is the story that Archduke Franz Ferdinand had traveled to Bosnia to see the centerpiece, which had resurfaced and was being displayed in a museum. It was this visit and his subsequent assassination that sparked the first world war. When its presence in New York became established it's what ignited a bloody battle for ownership between the Infidels and the Mescaleros. The Mescaleros used a folk magick charm called a Witch's Ladder which is made up from knotted hair or cord as part of a spell. It was their sorta trademark. The number of knots in the ladder dictated the strength of the spell. They took to leaving it at the scenes of their battles with the Infidels as a calling card. I've got a picture here somewhere." He roots around in his desk and eventually retrieves a dusty book and shows us a photo of a piece of cord with hair and feather knotted into it. I think he can see that we're far from impressed. He coughs and puts the book back.

"The Cruthers became the latest in a long line of people associated with the panel to mysteriously disappear. The window was in the perfect location to remain hidden, on a secret forgotten floor.

"I wish you luck if you're hunting the centerpiece," he adds with a smirk, before—somewhat dramatically, even for him—warning, "No good can come of it."

CHAPTER TEN

New York, 1904

"We have a rat in the organization." Milán had waited until he and Jan were behind closed doors to tell his brother.

Jan breathed deeply before speaking. "How can you be sure?"

"I have my ways, and the Mescaleros are always one step ahead of us."

Jan crossed his arms. His brother had been right too many times for this to be paranoia. "I'll deal with the rat."

"Keep your counsel. I don't know who it is yet, but I have my suspicions. I want you to keep your eyes open. I will be away for a few days."

"Where are you going?"

"Information has reached me not only that the mystic Nestor is alive, but also where he can be found."

"Let me go," Jan urged.

Milán considered for a moment. He couldn't really afford the time to go in search of a near-mythical figure, but his brother's methods weren't the most subtle. "No, it must be me." He tapped his brother on his shoulder. "I need you here to smoke out the rat."

*

Milán tracked Nestor down to the scorched sands of Joshua Tree. The surroundings were an apt location to find an old man of magick. The palette of the landscape was a washed-out stretch of reds, yellows, and purples. Misshapen cacti stood sentry throughout the desert, casting long shadows. They seemed like gnarled, unearthly creatures frozen in a march across the sands.

Milán found Nestor tending to a campfire, dressed in animal skins and a multicolored knitted poncho. His snow-white hair was pulled back in a ponytail, and bright blue eyes shone out of a deeply lined, leathery face.

"Master Nestor?"

The old shaman didn't look up from the fire but nodded.

"I've come—"

"Your name is Milán Cruthers. You've traveled from Manhattan. You and your brother own the Grand Hotel, and now you seek the doorway to World Ash."

Milán was opened mouthed in admiration for Nestor. "Truly your powers are mighty."

Nestor nodded again. In fact the owner of the Arkum Occult bookshop in the Lower East Side had been in touch and told him that Milán was asking about him. When he discovered that Milán wasn't a debt collector and that he might be able to benefit financially he had let himself be found. After a lifetime of adventures, he just wanted a quiet life, living in a small but comfortable shack.

"I can give you what you seek, but it may cost you…" Nestor gave him a sideways glance.

Milán took a deep breath and straightened his back. "I am prepared to pay the price."

Nestor named a figure.

"Oh, *money.*" Milán seemed disappointed that he was not being asked to endure a rite of passage, and handed over a thick wad of dollars.

Nestor took the money and quickly hid it within the folds of his poncho. "Yes, I've traveled to the realm of World Ash and I'm one of the few to return."

This was true. It had come about almost by accident when he and Talbot had been experimenting with occult rituals. Nestor had spent two and a half minutes in the other realm, but that had been two and a half minutes too long. That short time had shown him what a truly terrifying place it was. While Talbot kept the portal open, he had run back, tripped, and fallen back into this world. And when Nestor returned, he was different: he had *the glimmer.* He was able to hear dead people and have direct contact with them; and that became even stronger if he was given an object connected with them. The relentless babble drove him to the edge of madness.

Nestor may not have survived if his abilities had not faded over time.

"Tell me all you know," Milán asked with a hungry look in his eyes.

"First I shall sing you this song."

Nestor had a voice like sandpaper and Milán soon became impatient with the shaman. He'd shown him some courtesy by listening to his ramblings. Milán knew he was close to finding the doorway but was missing the final part of the jigsaw.

"Please, Master Nestor, I have traveled throughout this land gathering the knowledge to get to World Ash—"

"Hush! Listen to the night…" Nestor narrowed his eyes, but with a sideways glance he realized that this was one evasion too far. "There is a wall on the forbidden floor—you need to use the knowledge you've gathered to find the spot—where the membrane between our world and World Ash is thinnest. The whole of that building is constructed just to enable the energy to flow to that spot. You must build a window in that wall. It's a wall which doesn't face out, but this will be a window which looks out into World Ash."

Nestor brought a crumpled piece of paper from within his seemingly voluminous poncho.

"You must create the window to this precise design. The final segment to be included is the most important one; this *must* be installed last. It is the Baphomet centerpiece."

"The Baphomet centerpiece doesn't exist. It's a myth."

"It does exist. It's very real, but it won't be easy to come by.

Without it you might be able to get to World Ash, but you could never return…"

"Do you know where it can be found?"

"No."

"In that case how did *you* do it?"

"That was tied up with the rituals and knowledge of Talbot and that knowledge died with him."

"How do you know about the window and the centerpiece?"

"My visit to the other realm set me on a path for the next few years. It obsessed me. I needed to know if there was a way back to World Ash, on a similar path to yours."

"And with this window we can get to World Ash and harness its powers?"

"No. For that there is a book, a very old book of ancient rituals and incantations. They are at their most potent when they are chanted by someone with *the glimmer*."

"Yes, I understand."

"The book has been passed down through generations of seekers of the hidden realms. It is said to have come from the ransacked libraries of—"

"Fine, fine, how do I get the book?"

"For a small sum I can let you have it…" The old shaman worried that he'd pushed too far.

With no flicker of emotion, Milán reached into his jacket, brought out more money and handed it to Nestor.

"Follow me and I'll give you the book. But first, a warning. Two people with the glimmer must *never ever* chant the incantations at the same time: that would unleash a terrible power that cannot be controlled in our world."

Milán followed Nestor across the desert until they got to his shack.

"Wait outside."

Milán bowed his acceptance. He was more used to giving orders, but he allowed this from the old shaman.

Nestor found the book on his third attempt. He blew the dust off the cover and gave it a rub with his elbow. The small book was not much to look at—a brown leather cover with no writing—and gave no indication of the real, terrifying power and knowledge contained within its pages. But the truly powerful never do. Nestor put his palm on the cover and had a moment of indecision.

He looked at the book and then toward the door. He knew Milán's type; what was he doing passing this knowledge to such a man? He could hand the money back and claim to not be able to find the book, then burn it after his visitor had left. No, that would never work; Milán would never believe him. Caught on the horns of indecision, Nestor got a whisper, his first in years. He saw the unfolding consequences of handing the book over, and he smiled. It would not be the worst thing in the world if the Cruthers brothers were to mysteriously disappear.

Nestor opened the door.

"Sorry I was so long. I eventually—"

Milán almost snatched it from his hands, a smug, satisfied

look on his face. He didn't say another word but bowed in front of the old shaman.

Nestor watched him walk away across the desert, now tinged a deep copper with the setting of the sun.

The brothers and the sinister realm of World Ash deserved each other.

CHAPTER ELEVEN

The journal of Mary-Jane Mountmore

They are hunting me through this dark corridors, this forgotten, damned place. They are closing in. I'm running out of places to run. I can't allow Miles to get hold of the Baphomet centerpiece, not now that I know what it can do.

It was like a whirlwind, for a while it felt like I almost lost my mind being with Miles. It was a blizzard of parties and people. He was good to his word. He introduced me to producers and directors and helped me get auditions and start to network. I began to feel a glow of optimism for the first time since I arrived. Maybe I did have a future?

I fell for Miles's shabby glamour and charisma, and he swept me off my feet. Now I know he had ulterior motives, and not the usual that a girl would expect.

One day, he showed me a room in the Cruthers called the Minty Library, which has an unusual fireplace: ornate, with serpents and trees in black metal relief and asked me what I thought of the fireplace. Odd question. I ran my fingers over the cold metal and told him I thought it was very tactile. I said that I thought that there was *other* about the fireplace…It's a doorway and a safe? That can't be right.

He gave me an odd look, didn't say a word, and left.

When we were lying in bed one morning, he told me that I have *the glimmer*; he knew because he has it, too.

I didn't have to ask him what that meant. I guess I'd always known it: I'd always heard *whispers*; I saw shadow people that others didn't see.

He said he could help me harness and strengthen my abilities.

"Hey, honey, I think my abilities are pretty strong anyway," I'd said, pushing my shoulders back and chest out, but only got a weak smile in response, so I just accepted his offer.

Of all the men I've met, he was the most difficult to read. Men are usually very simple creatures, but his mood could spin on a dime. Soon he became jealous of my growing abilities, and maybe a little scared?

Then Miles brought me into the Infidels' "parties". I was very wary about what kinda parties these would be. I had my keys ready between my knuckles if it became a bit too frisky, but early on it became apparent it wasn't *that kind of party*. It was barely a party at all. I was the only girl there and the rest of the room was made up mostly of the men I'd seen with Miles in the bar. We mostly read from old books, and some chanted.

I should have been bored, but something chimed with me. Gradually Miles stopped calling them parties; he changed to refer to them as meetings, and then *coven* meetings. There was a small brown leather book that Miles read from. After my third meeting, the words he read started to affect the real world. A purple light hovered in the air, and I pressed my hands against the walls of the room and found they had become malleable, spongey. I should have been scared, but I was fascinated. If I'd known what was to come, I would have been terrified.

I also began to hear talk among the Infidels of the Cruthers and of their exile. I thought the brothers who'd given their name to the hotel were dead, but as time went on I began to suspect that there was a more horrifying truth behind what they were saying.

I have learned some skills. I'm able to conceal things in plain sight. It's a simple party trick. The key which unlocks the spell is a combination of my own making, a line said in English: "The last piece of the road, which leads to a place beyond the imagination of humans."

Spoke to Henry about the centerpiece. It can't fall into the Infidels' hands. It can't.

*

Marshall

Conner closes the journal.

"Useful. Any idea where she hid the centerpiece?" I ask.

"Well, no…"

"Great."

"But it mentioned someone who might."

*

We find ourselves sitting in the New York Public Library. It's one of my favorite places in the city. Every time I walk into the high-vaulted reading room I feel about twenty percent more intelligent, as though the knowledge from the years has soaked into the walls and radiated out to me. In a city with so much crammed in, it offers space and a little oasis of calm. With low-hanging beaux art chandeliers, and that mural on the ceiling, it almost feels like moving into a different, magical realm.

"Let me see." I look at the journal and Conner points at the last line again.

There was no way we were going running back to Faulkmeyer again, so it was time to do some research. It didn't take long for me to find the Henry she was referring to; there are hundreds of web pages dedicated to the Dark Orchid and they disagree with each other about most things, but they do agree that the Henry mentioned in the journal is Henry Nash. He was working at the Cruthers when they met, but he went on to become a senior professor at NYU, teaching Modern myth and legend. I didn't even know you could take that. Now he's in semi-retirement but is currently overseeing a social history project at the library.

I imagined he'd rebuff any requests to talk about the Dark Orchid, but while I was researching him I noticed that he had a new book out about occult sects in New York. , I contacted the university to ask for an interview with Professor Nash for our podcast. It took half an hour to create a shell site for the podcast—it would pass a cursory inspection but would collapse like rice crackers in the rain upon closer scrutiny. Amazingly we received a reply just half an hour later saying that Nash would be happy to do an interview later that day.

"Professor Nash will see you know." A smiling woman gives us directions.

We push the door open to a large office to see a man rubbing out some writing on a whiteboard. Behind him is a desk with papers, a telephone, and books on it. He must be nudging ninety but looks like he's in his sixties, a full head of white hair flecked with black swept back from his face, and a pair of glasses lodged on his nose. He's lean, and dressed in smart blazer, tie and slacks.

"Hello, Professor Nash. We've got a meeting?"

He looks away from the whiteboard. "Ah yes, the podcast. You want to know about my book?" He smiles while Conner and I exchange an uneasy glance.

"Well, sorta," Conner says unhelpfully.

"'Sorta'?"

"Err, yes, we've actually come here to speak about Mary-Jane Mountmore."

"Right." Nash's eyes narrow and his body stiffens. He looks at his desk and begins to edge toward the phone, I guess to ring security to get us slung out.

"We've got her journal!" Conner blurts out.

Nash stops in his tracks and moves away from the phone. "Okay. Can I see it?"

Rather hesitantly Conner brings it out of a pocket in his jacket and puts it down on the desk.

Nash glances down at the journal and smiles sadly. He traces a finger across the cover, opens it, and flicks through a few pages.

"I had such a massive crush on May. She knew, of course, and was very sensitive about it, very gentle, very kind. She took me under her wing. This city eats its young and it would have chewed me up and spat me out." He seems lost in his thoughts for a moment, then remembers that we're in the room and becomes more guarded. "How did you come by the journal?"

"I helped Mr. Goldstein—you might remember him as Gold—find his dog, and he gave it to us."

Nash raises his eyebrows. "He *gave* you the journal. He must really love that dog."

"That's we said," says Conner.

"How is the old shyster doing?"

"Ummm…he's dead."

"Oh."

Conner looks down at his sneakers, I look up at the ceiling, then all three of us look down at the journal.

Nash breaks the silence with a cough. "What's your interest in May?"

I get the feeling that if we called her the Dark Orchid be kicked out.

"We're Phantoms Inc."

"Of course you are," Nash says, stifling a laugh. I'd love to meet someone who doesn't do that. "And?"

"We think we've uncovered some new details about her murder and—"

"Okay, okay," he says, adding a heavy sigh. "You know, about every three years or so someone turns up saying the exactly the same thing. I will give this to you: you managed to get in front of me, and not many of them do. I'm going to have to have a word with the front desk. They're getting very slack. I think there's been new staff recently. Not their fault, I suppose."

Nash traces a finger across a page of the journal then closes it.

"I don't know what you want from me. Everything I know about May is out in the public domain. I wish it wasn't, but there you are."

"Not quite everything."

His eyes narrow again. "What do you mean?"

"We've read in the journal that Mary-Jane—May— said that she was going to tell you that she couldn't let the centerpiece—the Baphomet centerpiece—fall into the hands of the Infidels. She must have told you something."

Nash stares into space.

"You'd think so. It's seventy years ago, you know; I can't remember what I had for breakfast this morning…I'll tell you what I remember. We were at the Cruthers and the Infidels were closing in. heir coven leader, who May had a brief fling with, was hunting us down. She said that she was hiding it in plain sight. May didn't elaborate. It all got very messy very quickly and that was the last time I saw her. Now, please leave."

"Thank you, Professor Nash." I hand Nash one of our business cards. I have to get rid of them somehow. "If you remember anything else, get in touch." I feel like a proper detective saying that.

Nash peers at the card. I'm pretty sure that he's going to put it in the trash as soon as we leave.

Before we're out of the door, Nash has one last thing to say. "Oh, and…Boys, beware the Infidels."

"Why's everyone saying that?" Suddenly Conner's head yanks up. A as though he's being operated by remote control, he walks over to the journal, picks it up, and his back stiffens as though he's had an electric shock.

It's happening again.

*

Conner

One moment I have my hands on the journal and the next I've been transported to a grimy street. I can still see Marshall and Nash, but it's like there's a layer of gauze between us. My new surroundings look and feel more real to me.

I'm standing next to the heavy-set brother from the portrait in the hotel lobby. He's bobbing from one foot to another, like a bull about to stampede. He has five equally heavy-set men around him. They aren't aware that I'm there; these are just shadows of what's been. We are across the road from a shop with a sign that, between peeling paint, says "Arkum Occult." All eyes are on the shop.

"Are you sure that the centerpiece is in there, Jan?" one of his gang asks. His shaved head and thick neck give him the appearance of a hammer.

Jan nods. "Yes, Casteello, it's there. I want you flanking me when we go in." His eyes remain fixed on the shop across the road.

The shop front is browned with age and looks abandoned. I cross the road and head close to the window. There's a seemingly random collection of items on display, including an ornate silver compass and a shriveled, dried-up claw, which I eventually recognize as a monkey's paw. All covered in a layer of dust.

I'm joined by Jan and his five-man team. A faded, stained, unwelcoming "WE'RE CLOSED! COME BACK LATER" hangs behind the grimy glass. They try the door. It's locked but offers little resistance, and the men flood into the shop. I follow in their wake. Clutching knuckle dusters, guns, and knives, they had prepared themselves for many things; however, what they hadn't prepared themselves for was nothing.

The shop is deserted. There is a front desk, a cash register, and shelves lining every wall. The shelves contain books, and bell jars with things bobbing in liquid. Everything in the shop is covered with a blanket of neglect. The gang's entrance sends dust floating into the air, and all six of them have to fight desperately to stop themselves sneezing. When the dust has settled Jan gestures for his team to search the shop. Whatever their skills may be, but grace is not among them, and I'm treated to the sight of five heavily built men almost tiptoeing around an empty shop, treating items that look like junk as though they were precious jewels, while all the time trying not to sneeze.

After a few minutes of searching, the centerpiece is nowhere to be seen. Jan nods at one of his men and gestures toward a curtain behind the counter. The man nods back and walks through the curtain. Immediately there is a swishing sound, a strangled scream, and a loud thump. A second man, who had been ready to follow, hesitates, and they all looked at each other. Jan finds a long brass poker and brushes past the nervous men. Standing as far away as he can, he pushes the curtain aside with the poker. An unseen force shoves the poker with such force that it ends up embedded in the door frame.

"Shit!" Jan's Eastern European accent comes to the fore.

One of the men points to the floor. The first man has rolled back and is lying there. His head has been caved in, and blood pools around him from the wound. He's still breathing, but not for long. There is a crimson mark on the door frame with blood starting to run down; strands of hair and bone are entwined in the wood.

Jan and one of his men grab the poker and wrestle it out of the door frame. Working up from the floor, Jan waves the poker, trying to find out where it's safe. It is only when he gets to around knee level that the invisible force kicks in and pushes the poker out of his hand.

He lies down and crawls through the doorway and around his dying comrade while trying to avoid the blood. When he's put a body length between him and the doorframe he tentatively gets to his feet. When the others see that he is unharmed they crawl through to join him. I just walk through.

We find ourselves in a room as clean and ordered as the other one was dusty and chaotic. The walls are white and the floor is made up of dark tiles. The only other thing in the room is a finely detailed fireplace at the end of the room. It's just like the one described in the journal. The relief work looks weathered, in parts showing the metal underneath the paint, but the hearth looks gleaming and new. Something in the hearth is shining.

Jan rubs his chin.

"What's that?" one of the men asks, staring at the glinting light. I watch as he stretches his hand out toward it, almost as though he's hypnotized.

"No, don't!" Jan yells, but he's too late.

The man screams as a blue flame shoots out from the light and roars up his arm. Within seconds his whole body is consumed by flames. The others quickly step away from the burning figure, who collapses in agony to the floor. The fire burns itself out and leaves behind barely recognizable charred remains. One of the remaining men bolts for the door and Casteello runs after him, either to stop him or to escape himself. They both seem to have forgotten about the invisible force, which shoves the man to the side. He puts his arm up to protect himself and is knocked to the floor, unconscious but still alive. Casteello skids to a halt just in time.

A silence descends on the room.

Jan crouches in a fighting stance and circles the room looking for an invisible assailant. I can hear breathing, heavy in my ears. Jan must have heard this, too. He stands still and looks around.

"What—"

Jan holds his palm up to stop Casteello. He recovers the metal poker and tentatively pokes the fireplace with it. A tendril of blue light snakes out from the fireplace, along the poker, and up through Jan. He spasms but can't let go of the poker; his grip becomes tighter. The smell of burning flesh fills the room. Casteello knocks the poker from his hand. It goes clattering along the floor as Jan collapses. Casteello quickly takes his coat off to smothers the flames. With the coat around him Jan is curled up into a ball, his eyes are closed, and he clenches his teeth with pain, but can't prevent himself from uttering a grunt like an injured animal.

"Boss! Are you okay?"

Jan checks his pockets and brings out a phial of what looks like cocaine. He inhales it and, wincing, gradually pulls himself up onto his feet. Shaking his head from side to side, he begins to mutter a chant under his breath. Instantly, bright blue sparks fizz from his fingers and scurry like a spider around the fireplace. A bolt of energy from the fireplace meets the sparks, which crackle and flare, sparring back and forth until the sparks from Jan get the upper hand and glow around the fireplace, hiding it in a thick mist.

"Look!"

Jan looks at where Casteello is pointing. In the hearth, the mist evaporates to reveal the satanic goat of the Baphomet centerpiece. He smiles as Casteello stares at it. "We're taking that, and we're taking the fireplace."

"But how—"

A single look from Jan shuts down any protests. "I'll take the centerpiece, and you arrange for the fireplace to be brought back to the hotel."

Jan cautiously pads toward the centerpiece, takes a deep breath, clenches his teeth, and touches it with his fingertips, as though he's expecting a shock or that the goat might bite. But nothing happens. He picks it up and tucks it under his arm.

For a moment Jan looks around at his fallen men.

"That's the price that had to be paid. They knew the danger."

Cold, very cold.

Jan takes a deep breath, steps over the bodies, and leaves. I follow him out of the shop just as I feel myself being brought back to the here and now.

I fall back against the wall and Marshall rushes forward to help me, but what I've learned helps get me steady on my feet.

"I know where the Baphomet centerpiece is. We've got to get back to the Cruthers now!"

We thank a bewildered-looking Professor Nash and leave.

CHAPTER TWELVE

Murray

I didn't really realize the significance of the name when it was initially mentioned to me. I came in early hoping that I could get a march on the tsunami of shit that had come my way because of the business at the Cruthers, and now here is an extra bit of spice. As soon as Sergeant Boggart sidled up to me, I knew I was in trouble. His approach was heralded by the smell of chili dogs, and then there he was with a smirk on his oily face, which said that he was about to ruin my day.

"Okay, what is it?" I asked to get a jump on him.

"What?" But his smirk just got wider, and he followed up with "Henry Nash."

I shrugged. "Should that mean anything to me?"

Incredibly, the smirk got even wider, making him look like Jack Nicolson's Joker, and how I wish I'd savored those few moments before I knew what the name meant.

Five minutes later, I was arranging for Marshall and Conner

to be brought back in. I even suggested to the patrols where to look for Phantoms Inc. I'd laugh if it wasn't so grim.

I'm trying to piece together what happened. Henry Nash—a professor—is dead: sad, but hardly surprising as he was an old geezer. What *is* surprising is the manner of his death. He was dismembered in the New York Public Library. I've seen video footage of the crime scene and it looks more like a slaughterhouse than a place of learning. I'll visit later but I can tell from the blood splatters on the wall that it was a frenzied attack. The face has been slashed repeatedly so that you can barely tell that this was once a person. The body parts have been arranged in a very particular way, and I recognize the pattern between this murder and the infamous Dark Orchid murder, which my grandfather worked on. It doesn't take much digging to unearth a connection between Nash and the Dark Orchid, but what has pulled me into this is that, only two hours before the esteemed professor met his demise, he was visited by none other than Phantoms Inc.

Marshall and Conner are bundled into the station. The two officers escorting them are nothing but professional, standing just the right distance behind them and keeping a watchful eye on them in case they try to run. I don't think they would: it's not their style and they aren't really built for a dash.

I decide to take a different tactic this time and interview them together; see if that shakes anything loose from the tree.

"What is it about this time?" Marshall asks. "We just got grabbed off the street by your hired goons."

"Well, for a start, they aren't *hired goons; they* are professional police officers."

Marshall harrumphs, but I've got to say it's surprisingly good to see him again; I just wish it was under different circumstances.

"Henry Nash."

Marshall and Conner look at each other.

"What about him?"

I wait a minute before replying. "He's dead."

"Dead? How?" squeaks Conner, and from experience I know that his surprise is one hundred percent genuine.

I'm relieved. I didn't want it to be these two bozos. "We…He was fine when we left…I don't…" stutters Conner.

"Yeah cause, you know, there can't be…" Marshall, clearly flustered, shakes his head. "What I mean is, we…I…we weren't any…"

I actually feel sorry for them. It seems that what I've told them has sent them into a tailspin. I was going to show them photos of the crime scene, but from their reaction to me just telling them Nash has been murdered I don't think it would achieve anything useful. I put my hand up to stop any more yabbering and push myself back in my chair.

"Tell me in your own words about your meeting with Henry Nash."

They do, but they talk over each other, the account tumbles out nervously, and at one point Marshall punches Conner in the arm. God, I could really do with a cigarette. I'm scribbling down some notes with key times, when there's a knock at the door.

When I get up they are squabbling in whispers. I answer the door and it's the ever-smirking, punchable face of Boggart. I sigh—this ain't gonna be good news.

"Thought you'd like to know that the receptionist from the NYPL has been in touch."

His eyes dart around, and he does his annoying quiz show thing of pausing to see what your reaction will be.

"Yeah, and?"

"Apparently, just after your boys left"—*My boys?* He tilts his head toward the interview room—"Henry Nash went down and gave the receptionist a huge telling off for letting them in. So—"

"So, Henry Nash was still alive when Phantoms Inc. left."

"Phantoms what?" Boggart says, laughing.

I shake my head to let him know not to go there. t doesn't absolutely rule them out: they could always have doubled back and murdered Nash. But I don't think these two are that devious, and I'd be straining to get a clear motive for them. I'm sure it won't take much digging to find out where they went next."

"Thought you should know."

"Thanks," I say through gritted teeth. I hate being grateful to Boggart, but I am glad that they are—temporarily—off the hook.

I walk back into the room.

"No, you shut up," Marshall says to Conner, who nudges him in the side, and they both shut up.

"Well, well, Phantoms Inc." And despite myself I start laughing. "Sorry, I didn't mean to do that."

"Don't worry, we get that a lot," says Marshall.

"I just have a last few questions."

"And then we're free to go?" asks Conner.

"Possibly. "

"Yeah, you've said that twice already," says Marshall, I choose to ignore him.

"After you left Nash, where did you go?"

"We went back to the Cruthers Hotel," Marshall replies.

"And that can be confirmed?"

"Yes, Atherton—the new manager—saw us."

I scribble the name down, and I know that just an hour from now I'll be squinting at my barely legible note trying to work out what it says. I'm pretty sure it's gonna check out, but I still frown and tap my pen on my notepad. "And he'll confirm this?"

Another look between them, which I can't read.

"Well, the guy's a prick"—this gets a nudge in the ribs from Conner—"but yes, he'll confirm we were at the hotel later that afternoon."

"Okay then, you're free to go. But you remain persons of interest."

"What does that mean?" Conner asks, then chews his lip.

"It means that we'll be keeping a close eye on you and will pull you in for further questioning if we need to. Again."

Marshall is out of his seat before I've finished the sentence. "We'll remember that." He's dragging Conner up and out. Just before he leaves, he gives me a cheery wave. Oddly enough this convinces me that they aren't behind the murders. No one who has perpetrated such horrific crimes would be *that* idiotic.

Next order of business is to visit the Nash crime scene, but after that I am visiting the Cruthers Hotel. Phantoms Inc. might not actually be behind the murders, but something tells me that, if I keep a close eye on them, they will lead me to who is.

*

Marshall

"We've got to get back to the apartment."

"Why?" Conner asks.

"'Cause my hair is a mess." He rolls his eyes. "Plus I think there's most of a burrito left in the fridge. I could eat my own arm off."

"How can you think about food at a time like this? We've got to find the centerpiece!" Right on cue Conner's stomach rumbles.

"Okay, I'll give you that. We'll go back to the apartment, quick pit stop, then back to the Cruthers."

We barrel back to the apartment swerving between street people, psychotic cyclists on the sidewalks, and tourists. I really need to put some deodorant on; I'm sweating profusely from our jog across town. We have to navigate through the maze of hipsters in Donkey King to get to our apartment, and there, outside our door, is a package. It's got "Phantoms Inc." written in blue pen across the front, with no sign of postage. It's roughly A4 in size and looks like it could contain a book. We look at each other, then at the package.

"We could ask Klaus who dropped it off?" Conner says, and I notice he takes a step back.

"We don't have time." I pick it up. "Well, it's not ticking." I unwrap it. There's a letter and a hardback notebook with a scuffed and faded green cover. I quickly scan what's written

It's a letter from a dead man.

CHAPTER THIRTEEN

I show Conner the letter from Henry Nash.

Conner and Marshall,

I have had time to think about our conversation, and it's important that you know the events of the final evening and the Infidels' involvement, and especially that of Miles Hamer, their coven leader at the time.

The last time I saw Hamer was in the bar, only minutes after May left. He arrived with his cronies and nearly knocked me off my feet as he tried to breeze past me, and only stopped when I shouted to ask if he was looking for her.

He spun on his heels and ran straight at me, all pretense of civility fallen away. He grabbed me by my throat and pinned me to one of the pillars, demanding to know where she was. He was a lot stronger than his willowy body would suggest.

I could barely speak but pointed in the opposite direction to where she'd gone. It wasn't much but it would buy May some time. Miles dropped me and ran in the direction I'd pointed. As soon as I caught my breath, I left the Cruthers. I've never been back, and I never saw any of those people again.

The Infidels went to ground again and became the stuff of myth and legend, the equivalent of the Jersey Devil or the Illuminati—anything mysterious that happened in NYC, they'd be behind it. The truth is a little more nuanced, I feel. From my research, the Infidels became scattered and little more than petty criminal gangs. Nothing's been heard of them for over a decade. As for Miles, as far as I've managed to ascertain, he had an ignominious end. He'd come from a wealthy family, and they used their connections to get him out of the country. Rumors are that he died of hepatitis ten years later in a tiny village in Italy, reduced to poverty and an addiction to opium.

You asked me about the Baphomet centerpiece, so I assume you already know about the Mescaleros. Their story is a bit more involved. Although they had gained the much sought-after *and blood-drenched centerpiece during their war with the earlier incarnation of the Infidels, it didn't bring them what they desired. The leader of the cult took it from the Cruthers Hotel the night the brothers disappeared. Bad luck followed him and the centerpiece. The Mescaleros were decimated through a series of seemingly unrelated events— illness, accidents, and random attacks—all in the space of a few hours. Casteello hid the centerpiece and fled New York, never to be heard of again. It was assumed that Mescaleros would simply end when Casteello fled but—much like the Infidels— whispers of their continued existence persisted throughout the years. I've detailed in this in my latest book.*

I enclose the notebook that came to be in my possession through a convoluted set of circumstances. It is reputed to have been found with Miles Hamer. I can't vouch for that. Certainly the handwriting at the start resembles his, but then it descends into gibberish. I hope it is of help.
Henry Nash.

"What do you think?" I ask Conner. He shrugs.

"It's worth a go." and takes the notebook in his hands and a shock runs through his body.

"I'm in a dark room.", he says in a faraway voice.

*

Conner

Miles Hamer's body is wracked by a pounding cough so hard that it makes the springs on his bed squeak, the gun falls out of his right hand, and the needle out of his left. The cough gradually abates. The threadbare curtains are pulled shut on the windows, which rattle in the wind and threaten to shake apart, the glass only being kept in place by tape.

"Oh man…" he rubs away tears with his dirty and frayed shirt sleeve, then clutches his sides.

That cough had felt like it dislodged something. I now sense his tongue flicking around his dry, cracked lips, finding a new sore, which he probes, tasting an acidic tang.

He reaches across to retrieve the tequila in the finger-smudged glass and knocks the contents back in one gulp. The liquid has an oily taste, its welcome sting putting his—my—teeth on edge but knocking back the other pain. Hamer reaches for a green hardback notebook—*this* notebook—and a pen. He opens the book but his hand is too unsteady to write. He throws the book and pen to the floor and I can feel his frustration. Each day seems to bring a new addition to the pain party, and his skin has gained a yellow pallor.

Putting down the glass, he reaches for the gun, and his hand trembles. Hamer closes his eyes, breathes deeply, and clenches and unclenches his fist to stop the shaking. He has to do it six times before the trembling calms down but there is still enough of a shake that he has to rest his hand on his bony knee to steady it and aim the gun at the door.

Something is coming for him, laughing in the shadows, and tugging at his dreams, ready for a reckoning. Well, he isn't going down without a fight. He sees something out of the corner of his eye, in the corner of the room, scuttling, and swings the gun round, only just stopping himself wasting a bullet on a cockroach. Miles lets out a high-pitched laugh, which verges on the hysterical, seconds away from crying. He shakes his head from side to side to clear it, and again steadies the gun—as much as he can—and aims it at the door. After several minutes of quiet he turns his sunken, red-rimmed eyes to the cracked clock next to the tequila bottle. It shows just after half past three. He groans; another three hours till dawn. It feels rare that he has gotten more than half an hour's sleep in one stretch.

Miles's head jerks up. The clock now reads half past four. His gun isn't in his hand. Oh God, is that door open? Is there light streaming in? Where's that coming from? He hunts frantically for the gun, expecting to be pounced upon any minute. I feel his warm wave of relief as he finds the gun tangled up in the stained bed sheets, and sets himself back up in his sentry position, guarding the door.

As he waits, I can hear his thoughts as if they were mine. No one would believe him about what happened that night at the Cruthers, and he's been cursed ever since.

He had tracked down Mary-Jane—May—and backed her into a corner with a blood-red intent in his heart, but before he could act up his intentions, a crackle of energy had erupted from the window. It had flown around the pair of them, needling and pushing them. He—*I*—can still sense the burning feeling as the energy raced around his body. He heard May scream and saw her being pulled toward the window. For a split second he saw two Mays: one was the fully solid, physical May; the other was a transparent purple after-image of her. The purple after-image was sucked through the window, leaving the physical being to be whipped and shocked by the energy. It burned an angry crimson and tore through May.

I can feel the lingering horror in Miles, who could only watch as May screamed, the energy tearing her in two at the torso. He saw her fall, bleeding and twitching, to the floor, her blood pooling around her and soaking into the carpet as the life drained from her eyes. I can feel, as he recalls it, the rope of energy that shot out from May's remains and lassoed him. He struggled against it but could already feel it cutting into his sides as it drew him closer to the window. The harder he struggled, the tighter its grip became. In his desperation he had recited an incantation, the first one that had come to mind. He could feel the air on his skin as the energy cut through his clothes, and the warm trickle of his blood down his body as it cut into his sides. At the same time it had felt like he was being wrenched out of his body, floating above himself, and I could see the look of agony on his face as he frantically muttered the incantation, sweat rolling down his skin. With a loud CRACK! the energy had disappeared, leaving Miles to fall gasping to the floor like a fish landed to shore. He had clutched his sides in pain as May's blood seeped toward him. Closing his eyes and gritting his teeth Miles had managed to push himself onto his knuckles and then upright, swaying uneasily, as if he could pass out at any moment.

As he remembers it, I can feel the shock of pain as Miles had pressed his hands into his sides and how this helped clear his head. He had to get May's body out of there, and he had to get away. Then he had heard the laughter. Deep, guttural laughter. He had spun around but there was no one there. Just for a moment he'd thought he could see, through the window, a goat-like creature, and had instantly broken into a burst of activity. He had rallied the rest of the Infidels to move the body and clean the area up as best they could. They hadn't needed to be told; they knew that they had to go to ground. They had spread themselves out to the four winds, only one staying in New York, deep underground.

Miles escaped the Cruthers Hotel, but the shadows had chased him wherever he went. As the months had progressed, so had the anxious, creeping feeling that something had been released from the window. He had increasingly felt that he was being played with, the way a cat plays with a mouse, and that eventually it was going to pounce. Lately he'd been seeing more shadows and hearing voices and laughter—which no one else could hear—more often. Time was running out.

Miles looks over at the needle, the only thing that helped to banish the shadows and provide some relief, at least for a short time. But even that has started to become less effective.

He is seized by another fit of coughing, and it takes a while to get the shaking under control. All the time he—and I—can hear the low, mocking laughter. Miles reaches for the needle and loads it with everything he has. He pulls a belt tight around his arm and injects himself. I can feel the same instant fire and comfort as I watch his eyes roll back in his head. His mouth drops open and his body slumps into the bed. The needle falls from one hand, and the gun from the other. I sense his heart stop shortly afterwards. His body wasn't found for another four days.

CHAPTER FOURTEEN

Marshall

Conner slumps against the wall, and I quickly take the notebook off him before it falls to the floor. I open the door to our apartment, help him in, and settle him on the couch, avoiding some action figures but not the stack of *The Tomb of Dracula* comics. He doesn't seem to mind. I make him a cup of coffee, and while he recovers I wolf down the burrito from the fridge and get Conner a banana, which is about a day away from going bad. I zip around the apartment, slap on some deodorant, gargle some mouthwash, and get my hair into some kind of shape, then dash back to get Conner, who's regarding the last bite of the banana with some suspicion.

"You ready to get moving?" I ask.

"Not real—"

"Great! Let's go!"

I set the pace but do have to stop every once in a while for

Conner to catch up. Finally, we get to the hotel and stand in the reception area. I wait for Conner to catch his breath.

"Where now?"

Conner points to the right and I start walking. He catches up, then overtakes me and leads us to the Minty Library. I look around the musty, wood-paneled room. I haven't been here for a while—things to do, people to see, secret bases to find—and it's usually out of bounds. I think NecronomiCon used it once when a Lovecraft scholar dropped by to do a panel because the surroundings are suitably eldritch. It's a room that seems to be slumbering, and I have to say it is quite a push to call it a library. There are some leather-bound editions—nothing worth "liberating"; randomly, they are mostly about crop rotation, which I don't think has a huge fandom. The fireplace is striking, though, and just as Mary-Jane—or should I now call her May?—described in her journal.

Conner runs his hand over the fireplace. "The centerpiece is here."

I squint at it. "Really? It looks like a fireplace to me. A bit of a fancy one, but still a fireplace."

"She hid it in plain sight, remember! We need the key to unlock her spell. She put it in her journal. What was it again?"

I take the journal from my coat and trace my finger over the last page as I read it aloud. "'The last piece of the road, which leads to a place beyond the imagination of humans.'"

As I say it there's a deep sigh and, like a morning fog lifting, a satanic goat with a pentangle in the middle of its head comes into view.

"The Baphomet centerpiece! Holy shit!"

CHAPTER FIFTEEN

Murray

A crime scene is organized chaos. We try to put a layer of reason and organization over events that, by their very nature, are messy and upsetting. At first glance there doesn't seem to be much going on but, if you were to look under the surface, you'd see a frenzy of activity. And such is the case at the Nash crime scene. They've been waiting till I get there before they take away the body parts, which have been covered in a gray plastic sheet to provide the late Professor Nash with some semblance of dignity. I check that everything has been cataloged and photographed. When I'm completely confident that all the procedures have been followed, I allow Nash to be taken to the morgue.

There are blood splatters on the walls, which are still being photographed and will be analyzed back at the station. I'm more convinced than ever that Phantoms Inc. aren't capable of this. Not this frenzied attack. It looks like the work of an animal, but there's some jarring elements, such as how the body parts were arranged. Now that I've seen it for myself, I'm sure that it's a copy of the Dark Orchid murder. I'll have to check when I get back to the station.

I sidle over to the forensic guys, who are peeling off their suits and have boxed up their tests. They completed their work before anyone else was allowed onto the scene.

"How long before we get results back?"

"Hopefully forty-eight hours. We'll let you know. The only other person who had access to this room was the security guard and we've swabbed her. You'll have to get swabs from your boys so we can check against any matches."

Since when did they become *my boys*? But I don't question it. "Will do." If there's one thing I've learned in my years on the job, it's that you want to keep on the right side of forensics.

"Oh, we did find something a bit…odd. It was just above the victim's head."

"Where is it?"

"We've bagged it up, but here's a photo." The forensic geek picks up a nearby camera and scrolls though it until he gets to the object in question.

"What the fuck is that?"

He shrugs.

Great, another piece of the jigsaw puzzle that not only doesn't fit anywhere but seems to be from an entirely different puzzle. Now I've got to wait for the forensic results and figure out who would want to kill a renowned New York professor who should have retired years ago. There's also Angela Maron, the actress found at the Cruthers, and Goldstein. There's a lot of similarities linking these three crime scenes.

I've got somewhere to be as I mull over all these elements.

The Cruthers Hotel.

*

I'm still not sure about that gargoyle. It's leering down at me from the hotel, which, to be honest, is trying too hard. What's a gargoyle doing on a hotel anyway? Who would be impressed or intimidated by that? They should try manning the front desk downtown on a Friday night, then they'd know what real horror is.

I walk through its impressive but tarnished doors. The Cruthers Hotel has certainly seen better days. Just about everything in the place seems so *tired*. The carpets are threadbare; in places the wallpaper is peeling. There's a white rectangle on one of the walls where a painting or a mirror once was, which highlights how the paint around it has yellowed with age.

The state of the place sorta makes sense, being in the throes of a contentious refurbishment. Even so, there's a melancholy feeling of neglect, like a family dog which isn't really being looked after. Yet underneath that sadness there's…something else? I've been around the block enough times to trust my sixth sense about a situation. I've walked into too many basements where everyone is acting casual just before it all explodes into violence, and that's what this place has got: that low hum of potential violence hiding in the shadows. As soon as you pet that neglected family dog, it bites your hand.

It's only when I think of hands that I realize mine has unconsciously drifted to my gun holster and the reassuring heft within. You never know.

"...and who are you?" A tall, ginger-headed man with a scrubby beard steps into view and glares at me. The expression on his face looks like he's just stepped in something on the sidewalk.

"You must be William Atherton."

He jolts backward, momentarily thrown. His eyes narrow. "Yes. Do we know each other?"

"No. I'm investigating a case involving Marshall Thompson and Conner D—"

"Ah yes! Phantoms Inc.!" And, God help us, we both laugh at the name, and somehow Atherton has managed to gain the advantage. "Yes, well, they aren't employed by me, and they have no direct link to the hotel."

Why is he so keen to distance himself from them? What's he hiding? "Okay, fine, I didn't ask if they were, but they have been here quite a bit recently. Did you call on their professional expertise for anything?"

"No, not really. Well, in a way. They've just been hanging about the hotel, really. Like a bad smell." He laughs at his own witticism. "I haven't really had much to do with them." And now he's looking over my shoulder as though I'm starting to bore him and he's searching for someone else to talk to. "It's our handyman Eugene who's been dealing with them, so you should speak to him."

"How do I find Eugene?"

"Oh, he's around." Atherton waves a hand in the air.

"What does he look like?"

"You can't miss him. Well, I suppose you could." He chuckles to himself. "He's about this big"—Atherton levels his hand around his knee—"and he's always wearing a tool belt—not that I've ever seen him make use of it, to be honest."

"So where would I find this munchkin with a tool belt?"

Atherton pauses a moment. "On the discovered floor."

"Eh?"

"Floor six and a half."

"Six and a half?" A half-remembered story floats to the surface. "Wait, is that the floor which was found—"

"Yes, that's the one. I can let you in there, I'm pretty sure that Eugene was taking Phantoms Inc. to the floor."

Atherton's whole demeanor has changed. He's no longer quite as pissy, and more cooperative. Is it because he wants to get rid of me? There's only one way to find out.

What Atherton failed to tell me was that there's very poor lighting. Luckily enough, I'd remembered to bring my flashlight—thankfully, I do tend to use it more than my gun.

I enter the floor and sweep the flashlight around. Man, it looks like they've had quite the party up here. It's littered with debris and smashed bits of furniture, and my boots crunch on the shards of mirror and glass. Huge lumps have been taken out the wall.

"Don't think much of your interior designer," I mutter under my breath as I pad around. It doesn't seem that anyone is actually on this floor. If Atherton has sent me here to get rid of me, I'll haul him down the station before can wave his hands around again.

My flashlight picks out something on the wall. At first I think it's a bit of graffiti, but when I get closer I can see that it hasn't been sprayed or painted. It's a gray bomb blast of two figures.

Now I want to get the hell out of here. I hear the sound of footsteps on broken glass behind me. I swivel around and aim my gun and flashlight in the direction of the sound, but I accidentally drop the flashlight

"Hello? Who's there?" I don't get an answer, but the noise of glass under foot just gets closer. Just as it seems I'm about to see who it is making the noise, the noise stops.

"I'm Detective Michelle Murray of the NYPD, please make yourself…"

I'm hoping that it's going to be Marshall or Conner. It's neither.

*

Marshall

"What do we do with the centerpiece now we've got it?" I ask.

"Errr…I think we've got to take it to floor six and a half."

"Are you sure?"

"Yeah, I think. Joey told me to find the Baphomet centerpiece, but Atherton told us it belongs on floor six and a half, so that's where we should take it. "

"Right then, let's do it."

"Okay then."

We both look at the centerpiece, but neither of us want to pick it up.

"Go on, then," I say.

"But I've got the journal."

"Okay then, but we can't just parade around with it…" I look around the library. Draped across one of the chairs is a dust sheet, which I take. I pick up the centerpiece, which is surprisingly light for its size and feels cold—I mean *really* cold, almost as though it's just come out of the fridge—and wrap it in the dust sheet, tuck it under my arm. "I want to get there without bumping into anyone."

Luckily for us no one is around and the way is clear for us to get up to floor six and a half. There's a low frequency humming, grinding noise, which is coming from the window and is getting louder.

"What do we do now?"

CHAPTER SIXTEEN

Conner

The noises in my head are overwhelming: maniacal laughter, racking crying, accusations. I've got to get out!

"We've got to get away."

"To where?"

"I don't know! Anywhere but here."

"Right! Right!" Marshall looks around. "Let's try one of the rooms; see if we can ride this out."

I feel too weak to offer any other suggestions. Marshall throws himself at a couple of doors without success. I can feel an almost magnetic force pulling me toward the window.

*

Marshall

It's like Conner's being operated by remote control. I chase after him until we find ourselves in front of the window.

It begins to glow and I feel its magnetic pull on the centerpiece. At first it's a gentle tug, like an insistent child trying to get your attention by pulling on your sleeve, but it soon becomes stronger, and stronger still the more I try to resist.

"Conner!"

He grabs me around the waist, which momentarily halts the movement, but then there's a sudden tug and the centerpiece flies out of my hand and is sucked into place in the window, like something being pulled into a plughole.

A bright light flashes out from the window and we both shield our eyes. A deep animal growl emanates from it, like a lion that's just claimed its prey. This is followed by a gust of wind so powerful that it knocks Conner and me off our feet and up against the wall. The low hum gets louder as the wind gets stronger. The debris begins to get caught in the wind. The sharp debris.

"We've gotta get out!" I shout at Conner. I try some more doors until one gives and lets us in.

The room smells musty. It's dark and I reach for my flashlight, which only adds an apologetic illumination. A groaning sound echoes around—probably pipes, but it sounds like the room is stretching and waking up. It takes some time before my eyes adjust enough to the gloom.

There are three individuals waiting for us. They are all men. And they are all wearing tracksuits: two in an unflattering purple, one in blue. The ironic thing is that the purple two don't seem to have seen the inside of a gym for a while, as they're carrying a few extra pounds. I guess the leader is the one in blue standing between them. He's got bad skin and a mullet haircut—which is the wrong side of Donkey King hipster and thinning on top.

"My name is Dwayne, like the Rock, and we are…" He sneezes and gets some toilet roll out of his pants and blows his nose. "…Sorry, this hotel is very dusty…And we are the Infidels!"

Conner and I start laughing.

"Oh shit! Thank God for that!"

"Stop laughing."

"Sorry! Can't! We've been told about the big bad Infidels and then you lot turn up!"

"Stop laughing. I'm warning you!"

"Oh stop! It's starting to hurt! Oh boy, I needed that!"

And that's when they bring the guns out.

"What the fuck is that?" I yell and point over their shoulders.

Amazingly, it works; they turn around and we run off, slamming the door behind us.

*

Conner

We're running out of options of where to run, but run we do.

"Where we going?" I ask Marshall.

"Uh, let's head for the staircase."

I haven't got any better ideas so I run after him.

"Phantoms Inc!" the Infidels yell with a mocking laugh.

They sound close behind us. And how do they know who we are?

Marshall throws himself at the door to the service stairs. But it won't budge.

Out of the darkness walks a man with half of his face missing.

"Where did he come from?" yells Marshall, as we look for other ways to escape the Infidels and the continuing maelstrom. We get battered about until we find our way into another room.

*

Marshall

"This doesn't look right."

We've entered a room which is far bigger on the inside than it is on the outside. It goes back *waaaaay* beyond where the room should stop, to the extent that we can't see the end, and there's that smell of burned toast again. We look at each other, look at the door, then look back. It's a choice between this room or outside with the maelstrom, the Infidels, and Johnny Half-face. None are great choices, to be honest.

"Let's explore." I wish I had the heft of the BPoD.

"Okay then," Conner says, with a quiver in his voice.

We head down the room cautiously, as though we're trying not to wake up a dragon—which might be the case. I'm getting the nagging feeling that this is familiar. Why is that?

We're two hundred yards in when the temperature

drops. We can see our breath turn to mist in front of us, and literally can't see the light at the end of the tunnel. Conner reaches out and touches the wall, then looks at his fingers. There's some kind of viscid liquid dripping from them.

"You know what? I'm gonna say that's not a good sign."

I remember why this is so familiar: we watched the latest 4K release of *Alien* recently. Oh dear.

Conner tries to wipe the goo off onto his jeans but only manages to get his hand stuck.

"That's not a good look…Hey!"

In the gloom I can see *something* on the floor, shuffling past my feet, but do I *really* want to see what it is? Oh God, I suppose I have to. It looks like…It looks like the roots of a tree creeping out toward me. I kick them away as though they were rodents, and a shiver runs through me.

"Should we go any further?" Conner asks.

Fuck no! Let's get the fuck out of here! Is what I want to say, but instead I go with

"We'd better had, cause"—I reach for a reason— "you know…" It's the best I can think of.

"Okay then," Conner says, minus any enthusiasm.

We creep slowly through the seemingly endless room. It's got even colder. As I watch my breath in the air I can see, beyond it, some other kind of mist.

"What's that?"

I'm pointing at some thin wafts of purple and blue light. It reminds me of the Aurora Australis that we were both lucky to witness recently. It's pretty much as cold here as it was there. Why do we always end up in places where we're freezing? Why can't we have a case in Puerto Rico or Mexico?

I really want to know that Conner can see what I can see.

"I dunno what it is."

Well at least he can see something.

"No wait, it's…You won't believe this…"

"Try me. I try to believe six impossible things before breakfast."

"It's the Dark Orchid."

"What?"

Before I can dig any deeper we hear a sound like a chicken leg being torn away from the body.

We turn and run.

For a horrible moment we're running as fast as we can but don't appear to be getting anywhere, but gradually the room comes into focus and we scrabble for the door and make our escape.

The wind is still bellowing through the corridor.

"Why did you run off? I don't understand."

We turn around and there's Johnny Half-face.

"Shit."

We turn and run the other way.

"Phantoms Inc., where are you?" Dwayne calls in a creepy sing-song voice from the other side.

"Fuck." And again, *how* do they know who we are?

We're running out of options.

"Why aren't you answering me? It's making me *really* angry!" Johnny Half-face yells.

"Shit."

"Marshall? Conner?"

"It's Eugene!" but he sounds like he's a thousand miles away.

"Which way now?"

"I don't know! This way!" I point down a corridor off at right angles and we run scared. I've got a vague idea that there might be another set of stairs, maybe leading to the roof. I don't know what else we can do. We pinball around the floor, and just when I think I know where we're going, we turn a corner and run into a dead end. The geography of the hotel seems to be shifting off, forcing us to follow a specific path until we're standing in front of the window. Of course we are. It's throbbing with power.

"This has got a horrible inevitability about it."

The maelstrom is at its strongest here.

The window seems to be standing out from the wall. It's almost...*alive*. I'm sure the goat in the center is leering at us. The whole floor is closing in.

"Conner! Conner! Stop!" Marshall is holding up his hand and I can see right through it, but I can't stop; I won't stop. I'm on a runaway train.

"Conner! There's got to be..." Marshall's voice is getting fainter as he fades away. I feel a flush of heat and see a blast of white light.

*

Dwayne

There are only two of them and there are three of us, so the math is on our side. I thought this would be pretty easy. But it ain't.

We should have had even more with us but two of the fellas canceled at the last minute. Waddya gonna do? We've been trying to get new recruits for a while but the young'uns ain't enthusiastic. The Infidels have all this history, but if it ain't on Tickity Tock *they* don't wanna know. I joined after I saw the group mentioned on a few forums. I just got back from a ban—all I was doing was speaking truth to power, but some can't handle it—which was fine 'cause I was thinking of leaving that forum anyways 'cause it had started to get overrun by those socialist snowflakes. Anyhows, I'd just logged on to see what the losers were doing without me and I saw a post about gaining back power and control. *At last!* I thought. For too long I've been kept down by the specialist interest groups who really run this country. That's when I found out about the proud history of the Infidels. Likes I said, there were more of us at first, but now it just seems to be us regulars. Oh, and our leader.

There's the three of us up here and before we know it Phantoms Inc. get away. I could kick myself. So, we start to hunt them down but it ain't easy. There's all kinds of madness going on and they manage to give us the slip. But then we catch a break and I hear some shouting coming from the direction of the window. We run in its direction, but before we can get there there's a blinding white light and suddenly everything goes quiet, the tornado stops, and all the debris falls to the floor. We round the corner to the window but we're too late. In front of us are two shadow bomb blasts.

"The boss ain't gonna be happy about that."

I point to what remains of Phantoms Inc.

CHAPTER SEVENTEEN

New York, 1914

They'd been waiting for him—of course they had. They'd let Jan and his men handle all the traps in the shop, and that's when they'd ambushed him.

Jan barreled into the hotel at breakneck speed, then skidded to a stop and hid behind one of the marble pillars as he spotted one of the Mescalero. He swore under his breath. The Mescalero took out a knife and sidled around the hotel reception. He was dressed all in black, had close-cropped hair, and a scar across his face. While he was looking the other way, Jan sprinted to the next pillar, he was just yards away from the stairway entrance. The Mescalero's head whipped around, and he began to walk toward where Jan was hiding.

Jan slammed into him, knocked him off his feet, and made a

run for the staircase. But he wasn't built for speed. His adversary followed close behind. Jan took two, sometimes three steps at a time in a bid to outrun him. He felt a sharp pain on his side and saw a circle of red spreading across his shirt. His adversary paused, which was all Jan needed; in one swift motion, he brought a knife out from his boot and planted it firmly in the Mescalero, who screamed as he fell backward, clutching at the fountain of blood erupting from his face and his face. He spasmed and was finally still.

Jan had no time to savor his victory. With one hand clutching his side, he hobbled up the remaining flight of stairs. He could feel his energy ebbing away. He didn't have long.

Jan fell with four steps to go until floor six and a half. Pain exploded in his head, perversely giving him a burst of energy. He dragged himself up the remaining steps and nudged the door open.

"Milán! Milán!" he shouted as he dragged himself over the carpet, leaving a trail of blood. He could hear the sound of footsteps coming up the staircase behind him.

Milán ran around the corner and was stopped dead by the state of his brother.

"Hurry!" Jan tried to shout but he was fading. "There are more coming!"

Milán ran to his brother and dragged him along the corridor. "How many of us are left?"

"Two? Three? They fought hard and well. They nearly bested us but…" Jan nodded down at the centerpiece clutched across his chest and smiled weakly.

"Don't try and speak. We are so close, so close!"

The brothers got to the window just as they heard the sound of a door crashing open followed by the sound of footsteps along the corridor.

Milán took care unwrapping the blood-soaked centerpiece to reveal the triumphant image of Baphomet. He breathed deeply and smiled. Finally, he'd done it.

"Brother, hurry," Jan said, his voice little more than a whisper, followed by a rattle. His eyes rolled around in his head and there was a gray pallor to his skin.

The centerpiece nearly slipped out of Milán's fingers, slippery with his stricken brother's blood. "Careful," he said to himself as he lifted it clear of its wrapping and felt a magnetic pull. It wanted to be part of the window! It knew where it belonged.

Jan lay slumped on the floor, his face white and his head lolling around as he tried to stay conscious.

Milán was sent reeling as a thickset bald man with a crooked nose collided into his side. They collapsed to the floor and fought. He pushed Milán aside, took the centerpiece and stood up.

"You." Jan pointed at Casteello, a drop of blood falling from his outstretched finger.

Casteello smiled, showing a gold tooth he'd got as a replacement for one lost in a fight – and clutching a Witch's Ladder he'd prepared for the standoff.

*

Casteello had been a good and trusted confidant of the Cruthers. Initially he'd supported Jan as an enforcer, his bull-like physique having been built up from working in the docks in Mexico after fleeing his home country of Brazil. When a turf war had broken out one night between the unions and local drug gangs, he escaped, covered by a tarpaulin in the back of a truck. He'd sought his fortune across the border, heading for New York, and again found work in the docks. That was where he'd first met the Cruthers. They'd been looking for some back-up muscle for a business transaction they thought might get a bit messy. It did, and the Cruthers—Jan especially—were impressed by his ruthless violence. He took no prisoners when he was breaking heads. Gradually he got more and more work from the Cruthers. He only ever spoke to Jan; Milán was always silent. Eventually he was working so regularly for the Cruthers that he gave up working at the docks.

He had risen through the ranks to become Jan's right-hand man. He'd also helped Jan with a piece of side business, dealing cocaine behind his brother's back. Casteello was aware that Jan himself indulged in the white powder. It was a useful piece of information that he had been sure he could use at some point.

The Cruthers had used Casteello to help set up sites for rituals and obtain objects to be used alongside their spell weaving. Jan had persuaded him to get involved. At first, he had gone along with it just to keep the brothers happy, but then, for the first time in his life, he had glimpsed something beyond his understanding, and he wanted to find out more. Casteello became enmeshed within the Infidels and their quest to gain entry to World Ash and the power it promised. He discovered an aptitude for learning the incantations and a hunger for the knowledge that the revered book, gained from the shaman Nestor, provided.

Casteello had not only survived but thrived by having a sixth sense when things were going down—it had got him away from the Mexico docks in the first place—and he'd sensed that the Cruthers were nervous and jealous of his growing power. So, way before the brothers had set out to ambush him, he had set up his own group ready to break away.

When he and the others had been summoned to an impromptu ritual at a new location, Casteello and his cabal had been prepared. The Cruthers'—and Infidels'—Achilles' heel was their arrogance. They had thought they could quickly snuff out the Mescaleros and, in a move typical of Jan, had tried to use violence and force to eradicate their rivals, but Casteello knew their methods and had been able to successfully fight them while staying in the shadows. In doing so, he had even been able to gain ground, culminating in sending a gang to face off against the Infidels on their very own patch for a final battle to decide who would gain dominion over World Ash.

*

Now here the three of them were, in front of the window for the final reckoning.

Milán leaped forward to grab the centerpiece. Casteello felt it being pulled from him, but not by Milán. It pulled away from both their hands and moved of its own accord. The Baphomet centerpiece hung in midair just in front of the window

"You're too late!" Milán crowed.

Jan smiled and, in a voice only he could hear said, "Brother, we did it…"

A white light blasted out of the window. Casteello fell back. When he propped himself up, all that was left of the brothers was a pair of bomb blast shadows. Dazed and not quite believing that the Cruthers had disappeared, Casteello gazed at the two gray outlines. Wisps of smoke drifted up from his clothes as though he'd been too close to an open fire. He patted them out and got to his feet to look at the leering goat with a pentangle on its forehead at the center of the window. Having checked that no one was watching, Casteello closed his eyes and muttered some incantations as he slid a knife around the edge of the Baphomet panel. A red glow emanated from the glass as he slowly removed it, its jagged edges cutting his skin. He smiled at the cuts. Casteello suspected that it wouldn't be easy, but he didn't mind the pain; after all those years, he welcomed it.

For a fleeting moment he thought he could see two figures tumbling as though they were falling down a well. But then they were gone.

With the centerpiece under his arm, he left the hotel and entered the night.

The three remaining Infidels, waiting outside the hotel, were no match for him. Adrenaline still coursing through his veins from his encounter with the brothers, Casteello sledgehammered them into submission using his fists, head and the centerpiece to slice through skin. Casteello laughed as he easily fought them off, leaving two lying in their own blood on the street while the other ran off into the night. It wasn't the first—and wouldn't be the last—blood the centerpiece tasted.

People stared at him and dogs strained at their owner's leads, snarling and barking, as Casteello passed by with the centerpiece under his arm. Winds began to whip around him, while the rest of the street remained calm. He knew he had to find somewhere to shelter. Looking up at the street name and remembering that there was a safe house close by, he put his head down and sped up.

Arriving at the house, Casteello fumbled with the key, shut the door behind him, and double locked it. He slept fitfully and, as the sun rose, left to take the centerpiece to his coven. He was triumphant to finally have the centerpiece in his possession but, after the events of the previous evening, he knew he had to get away as fast as he could. He hailed a yellow cab to take him to meet the others.

They had only been driving for only a couple of minutes when a truck came out of nowhere and only missed them because of the quick reactions of the taxi driver, who laughed. "Ha! You get used to that kinda shi—"

Smack! The windscreen cracked in a spider's web pattern as a bird slammed into it.

Disorientated, the driver crashed into a fire hydrant, sending a plume of water gushing into the air.

The driver was slumped, bleeding on the steering wheel. Dead or concussed, Casteello did not wait to find out. His door had buckled shut in the crash. After six kicks with both feet, it shrieked open and he leaped out, pushing the passers-by who came forward to offer help out of the way.

He had the centerpiece under one arm and used his other hand to wipe blood out of his eyes from a cut on his head. Casteello ran through the streets of New York avoiding falling trees and dodging street people who wanted to berate and attack him. He found a public phone booth and made sure he had his back to the wall, looking out at the street in anticipation of any threats that would come his way, tensed ready for fight or flight. He propped the centerpiece up against his leg. It might have been his imagination but he thought he could feel some heat emanating from it.

"Casteello? Thank God, I—"

"I don't have time. Gather the rest of the coven. My warehouse down at the docks; I'll meet you there in half an hour. I have the centerpiece."

"See you there."

Casteello decided it would be safer to cover the rest of the distance by foot. He was immediately aware there was a police car behind him, moving very slowly. He ducked into an alleyway. There could be any number of reasons why the cops would want to stop him; there was never going to be a good time, but today, especially, he wanted to avoid their attention.

He watched from deep within the alleyway as the cop car passed slowly, one of the officers looking around. Were they actually looking for him? He wouldn't take the chance. Casteello stepped over suspicious-looking bundles on the floor, passed by overflowing trash cans, looked around a corner, and saw the lights of the busy street he needed to be on. He picked up his pace only to find the light blocked out by a well-built man in stained white shirt and black work trousers. He had a confused look on his face, which turned to surprise then anger when he saw who was in the alleyway,

"Ah shit," Casteello whispered to himself, "Circo."

He had had some dealings with Anthony "Tony" Circo six months previously; he and his crew had been drawn into the war between the Infidels and the Mescaleros. Casteello had needed more old-school muscle and Tony had been happy to provide it. During one fight between the two sides, the Infidels had gained the upper hand and Casteello's men had beaten a hasty retreat, leaving Tony and his crew to the mercy of the Infidels. He had thought Tony had been killed in the skirmish—he certainly hadn't come looking for the money Casteello owed him—but here he was, very much alive. He *really* didn't need this.

"You know, I was just sitting two blocks away having a slice and some coffee, minding my own business, then the next thing you know I had this overwhelming urge to get up and come here. Didn't even finish the slice. And here you are," he growled. Casteello shifted from foot to foot to get a firm center of gravity and made his hands into fists.

"Here I am."

All too late, Casteello noticed the thick bike chain in Tony's hand as he ran toward him. Before he knew it Tony was on top of him. He felt the woosh of air as the chain missed his face by inches. Tony's shoulder nudged his own and sent him stumbling back against the wall. He managed to miss the next swipe of the bike chain, which took a chunk out of the brick behind him, but he dropped the centerpiece, which landed with a heavy thud. Tony dodged a punch thrown by Casteello, who then followed it up with a punch that landed in his stomach; there was no real force behind it, but it was enough to put Tony off his balance. Casteello swiped his legs around to try and take Tony's out from underneath him, a move he'd used down the docks when he'd had trouble. It usually worked, but it didn't now; Tony remained rooted to the spot and from his left boot he'd pulled out a knife, which he swung at Tony, catching Casteello on his face and barely missing his eye. The pain made him focus on the fight, but he was outgunned. He dropped to his knees as Tony raised his arm, ready to bring the bike chain crashing down on his head.

Casteello picked the centerpiece up with one hand, sprang up, and took a swing as if he were going to hurl it like a discus, aiming it at Tony's head. There was a crunch as hard glass met fragile skull; a gush of blood sprayed out as Tony crumpled to the floor. Casteello leaped over the body, soaking up the blood from his latest cut with his shirt sleeve as he ran toward the street. His bloodied, disheveled appearance barely got a second glance as he made his way through the busy New York street toward the docks.

Casteello was met at the warehouse by a group depleted by similarly freak accidents. He closed his eyes and clenched his fists at the news.

Blood dripped from the cut on his face onto the glass, which seemed to glow with pleasure. For a blind minute of red-hot rage he thought about smashing the centerpiece against the wall, but he took a deep breath and, instead, put it at the end of the room and swiftly walked away, as though it was going to bite him. All this time trying to get it, all the blood spilled, all the lives wrecked, and his only thoughts were to drop it into the sea or smash it into as many pieces as he could.

He and the remaining Mescaleros watched it cautiously.

"We can't keep it. It's cursed."

"What can we do?"

"Maybe we can find a way to harness its power?"

Casteello kneaded his forehead. Now that the adrenaline was wearing off, a whole world of pain was starting to creep up on him.

"We can't take it back to the Cruthers," he said, "and we can't move it from here."

"What can we do?"

An idea came to him.

"We can use incantations to lock it in time in this place, to a point a second into the future, so it will always be just out of reach for anyone looking for it and unable to influence anything in our world. There it shall remain until we can regroup and plan our next steps."

Casteello and the remaining few Mescaleros prepared the space. They chalked a pentagram around the centerpiece, with a line of salt circling that, and took six black candles from a bag. They placed the candles on the outskirts of the salt and lit them along with some incense. They joined hands, closed their eyes, formed a semi-circle facing the objects, and began to chant an incantation in unison. Loud to being with, the words filling the room; as the phrases were repeated, their voices became gradually quieter until they formed a low drone. After ten minutes, the centerpiece started to become opaque - before it disappeared entirely.

"Let's scatter. We all need to get out of town and go to ground. I'll be in touch when I work out what we do next."

"How will you know where we are?"

"I'll find a way."

They left and went their separate ways, Casteello bowing his head and muttering an incantation of protection over the warehouse, which would put it in a state of grace for the next fifty years, preventing it from being torn down or altered.

Casteello found a public bathroom and cleaned himself up the best he could, then went and bought a map of the US from a bookshop. He unfolded it on a park bench, closed his eyes, and put a finger down on the map. Opening his eyes he saw that his finger had landed on Akron, Ohio. Casteello sighed. It would not have been his first choice—or even his third—but that was the point; it would only be for—he hoped—six months at the most.

Within two months he'd established a life in Akron, and after six months he was able to bring his wife, children and now grandchildren from Brazil. He hid behind the mask of suburban life and played the part of a family man with a nondescript job working in a garage fixing cars, which he found he had an aptitude for. Casteello always had the intention at the back of his mind that he would return to New York, retrieve the centerpiece, and take up where he left off. At first, even as he bounced his new grand-son on his knee, he had a knife taped to his calf, a gun within reach, and one eye on anything or anyone approaching. But the years layered upon years—more children, family barbecues—until the day when he wasn't playing the part of a family man anymore; he just was one. Gradually the memories of his occult adventures in New York seemed like nothing other than a fever dream.

Casteello knew he shouldn't have a favorite among his grandchildren, but May had a sparkle, a *glimmer* about her, and when he was babysitting her, he told tales of his time in New York.

Eventually Casteello forgot he was ever in New York. But a seed had been planted in the mind of the young Mary-Jane.

CHAPTER EIGHTEEN

Murray

I pick up my flashlight, and it shows a man in a black suit. His eyes are glassy and fixed straight in front of him as though he's sleepwalking.

"Sir? Please make yourself known."

He keeps looking ahead with no recognition that I've just called out to him.

"Excuse me, sir. Could you please…?"

He slowly turns around to look at me.

Half of his face is missing. His shirt is dark with dried blood. I'm so shocked that I almost drop my flashlight and gun, but I regain my composure, leaving the gun at my side but keep the flashlight up and shining on him. After all my time in this job it's almost like muscle memory, and I instinctively back away down the corridor.

"I don't know where I am," the half-faced man croaks, and I can see soft, liquid things moving in the gap in his face.

"You're in the Cruthers Hotel," I hear myself say. It seems absurd to be answering his question as though he's just asked me the way to Penn Station.

"The Cruthers Hotel?" He looks around as if he's just noticed his surroundings for the first time. "Yes, the Cruthers Hotel. I was…" A look of terror dawns in his eyes . "Oh God, I…" His hand moves up to his ravaged face but stops just where the devastation begins.

This is a genuinely unique experience for me. I have no idea what to do or how to handle this, so I fall back on procedure.

"Sir, please get onto your knees and put your hands on your head," I say raising and pointing my gun at him. I have no idea what I'll do if he complies, I don't even know if my cuffs will work on him.

"What? Why? It's starting to come back to me, why I came here. It was the Infidels; they brought me here."

The Infidels?

"I need to find them. They tricked me!" he shouts, and suddenly he's become very angry and starts to run at me. I don't hesitate and fire three shots into him, lighting up the corridor, the sound deafening in this confined space, leaving a ringing in my ears. The bullets hit him square in the chest. Kill shots. They knock him off his feet and back down the corridor. Smoke from the gun drifts across the space. The man lies still, whisps rising from the holes in his chest. Tentatively I edge closer to him, only to see him prop himself up on his elbows and get up as if he'd just slipped and fallen.

He blinks and then fixes me in his sights. "Now I'm *really* mad!"

Shit.

All my training, all my procedures go out of the window, and I turn and run. I don't know where I'm running; all I know is I need to get away from that dead man who won't stay dead.

I run down through the hotel and that's when it starts to get freaky. It's as if a breeze of sounds whirls around me, and I hear voices, just snatches of conversations, almost as though parts of messages were being played back randomly:

"Let's put the knives down…"

"Mary-Jane…!"

I spin around trying to find the direction that the voices are coming from, instinctively trying to aim my gun to cover me, but I can't pin down where. The voices seem to be swirling around me. Out the corner of my eye, I see movement. I catch the after-image of someone as if they've just flickered into existence for a second, before blinking out again.

*

Marshall

"What an incredible smell you've discovered!" There is a funky citrus smell which—perversely—makes me a bit homesick for our apartment.

"So we're not dead?"

"I guess not. We'd smell better if we were dead."

We find ourselves in what looks like a forest, but it's not like any forest I've ever been in. The trees are mangled and gnarly, almost as though they aren't really trees at all, just weeds that have got ideas above their station. There's a sickly yellow haze over the place. And there's that smell. The ground is uneven with rocks littered about in clearings between the wrong-looking trees. There are thickets of brambles with thorns that look as sharp as flick knives. This ain't the most hospitable of places.

I'm getting the horrible feeling that something or someone is watching us.

Behind us is a rock face on which we can see a shimmering picture, like a pond that's had a stone thrown in it. Eugene is gazing in and looking confused. We must be on the other side of the window. The image shimmers and disappears.

"Any idea?"

"What, about that smell?" Conner asks.

"Yes, but no…I mean any of this?"

Conner shakes his head.

"I'm guessing this must be that World Ash we've heard so much about. Man, is it disappointing. Wait, what's that?" Conner leans down and picks a small battered book with a brown leather cover from the grass. He frowns, flicks through it, then pushes it into the pocket of his hoodie.

I put my hands up to the rock face and my fingers come away with the same viscid drool as it did in the impossible room. I wipe it on my jeans, but that doesn't seem to get it completely off. And these jeans were box fresh today. I thought I might run into Kim—you never know; I'm a glass-half-full kinda guy.

"You picking anything up?" I ask.

"Nope. It's gone really quiet since we got here. That's a good thing, right?"

I shake my hand. "Dunno. Could go either way."

From the depths of the wrong, mangled trees comes that sound again, like a tearing chicken leg.

"I think—" I start to say, turning around to Conner, but see him running away. "Oh, great."

I run after him. For someone who claims to have *occasional* asthma—like that's a thing—he can move pretty fast.

We must have been running for at least ten minutes—well, maybe five—before he stops. We find ourselves in a clearing. I wipe the sweat off my face as Conner catches his breath. I punch him in the arm.

"Sorry, I panicked."

"What's the plan?"

"I dunno. I'm new here myself."

I laugh. "You prick! Right, what we should do first is find Joey and Davey."

"I've got a thought."

"Makes a change."

"Charming. The panels in the window aren't random; I bet they're related to this forest."

"Right. Sounds reasonable. And?"

"Er, that's all I've got."

"Fantastic. Okay, so the panels in the window…what did they have?"

"That screwed-up castle."

"And that fucked-up tree," I add. "Let's explore and see if we can find either."

"That's hardly a watertight plan."

"You got anything else, mister 'the-window-panels-ain't-random' guy?"

Conner looks up into the air, narrows his eyes, excitedly points at me, then "…No."

"Then exploring it is."

I pick a direction and we head off. There are faint, disturbing, unidentified noises in the distance, but at least they're in the distance. We stay close together.

"Hey, maybe we'll find the Dark Orchid—May—here. So far, everything seems to have had some connection to her. Have you picked up anything more?" I ask Conner, as much to get his mind off what might be lurking in the forest; he keeps looking around with the trepidation on his face usually reserved for opening our fridge to find out what *that* smell is.

"I do know how she died, yes."

I punch him on the arm.

"Ow! That hurt."

"Shuddup, that's just a tickle. Why didn't you tell me?"

"Events sorta overtook us."

"Yeah, well, good point well made. So what happened? What did she say? Fuck! Did she say who, you know…" I slide a finger across my neck and stick my tongue out. I thought it might make Conner laugh. It doesn't.

"It wasn't a *who*, it was a sort of energy bolt from that window. It cut her in two"

Which kills the conversation.

We're walking along a path through a tunnel created by the mangled trees, shielding out the sickly yellow light. Gray, knotted, and seemingly riddled with tumors and leaking sores, they are leaning across like they want to hug each other. Conner and I try to keep away from them, but it's not easy and we keep bumping into each other.

"Stop it!" he says, pushing me.

The tree branches sway in the breeze.

I realize that there is no breeze. "Let's pick up the pace!"

We fall into line with that lolloping, awkward half-run-half-walk thing we do, which ain't elegant, but no one's watching. Hopefully.

The path seems to have been created by something having crashed through here some time ago: something big, something *very* big.

We eventually get to the end of the tunnel. I don't know if we see *the* fucked-up tree, but we see *a* fucked-up tree. And trapped in it is Davey. He is enmeshed in a twisted mass of roots, branches, and vines; one is wrapped around his neck and there is an ugly red mark underneath it.

I take no delight in finding him looking this wretched. Well, maybe I do. A tiny bit. Not much. He looks completely different from the sharp, confident Davey I'm used to seeing. He's very pale, and there are dark lines under his eyes. Davey's head is lolling about; it looks like he's trying to wake himself up. He slowly raises his head and squints his eyes as he tries to focus on me. I must finally swim into view 'cause he mutters, "Oh Christ, just my luck."

"Happy to see you, too."

"Get away from here while you can," he groans, "before *they* come back."

"Before *who* comes back?"

"The Cruthers, or what they've become."

"What do you mean?"

He shudders and the branches get a little tighter around him.

"There's a creature. A huge goat creature. It's the Cruthers."

"How do you know it's them?"

"It—they—spoke to me." It looks as though he's about to cry. "Then it took Joey."

"Do you know where it took her?"

"No, but it said something about a castle."

"It's got to be the castle in the window."

We try to loosen the vines to get Davey from the tree, but they only tighten, almost as though the tree is holding a gun to his head. The vine around his neck begins to tighten, choking him. Davey's eyes bulge, his fingers grasp desperately at the vines, trying to find some way to loosen them, and he goes red in the face. The tree only loosens its grip when we step away.

"If it wanted me dead, I'd be dead by now. You've got to find Joey."

Now, I do feel genuine pity for Davey. I don't want to leave him, but I know we must.

"We'll be back," Conner says, but I know he's not sure that we will be.

*

Davey

I've had a lot of time to think.

I know that Phantoms Inc. hate me. I don't blame them. I've probably given them more than enough reason to over the years. Fear and anxiety are constantly snapping at my heels, and the monster of my ego makes me do idiotic and hateful things, all leading to me being right here, strangled by a fucking tree. It's not the way I wanted to go out.

I knew we were out of our depth the moment we walked into the Cruthers and met William Atherton. I thought I could talk and charm my way through the situation—that normally works. It was a big deal. I knew it would do our profile huge amounts of good, but I could see that Joey wasn't coping well. She didn't want to be in there, but I bullied her into doing it. I've always had a gut-twisting feeling that one day our luck would run out, and maybe deep down I knew this would be the day.

*

"Spirits Unlimited?"

"Yes indeed."

The new manager of the Cruthers had short ginger hair, a

scrubby beard, and a look on his face like there was a bad smell in the room.

"Thank you so much for hiring us."

There was a slightly shocked look on his face as if I'd said something untoward about his grandmother. "It wasn't my idea, but at this point I'm willing to give anything a shot."

"Oh right. What's the problem?"

"You know about the discovered floor?"

"Floor six and a half?"

"We prefer to call it the *discovered* floor."

I'm sure you do.

"There have been some…incidents on that floor." He waved his hand in the air and I knew I wasn't going to get any more details. "And I've heard that you're experienced in dealing with such matters."

We were shown up to floor six and a half.

Usually when we get called in for something like this it turns out to be a job for a plumber, 'cause the odd noises and strange temperature drops are to do with bad pipes in the wall. But as soon as we got to floor six and a half…

"Give me a moment." Joey was doubled up against the door, clutching onto the frame to stop herself falling over, as if someone had punched her in the stomach. God help me, but my first reaction was annoyance: what a time to get cramps!

"Come on, you'll be fine."

She hobbled in, gritting her teeth as she stood upright. "You don't understand." She looked close to tears. "This one is *real.*"

"We can sort this out. We just need to find the center of this."

I tried to bulldoze our way through, the way I always do and the way that's always worked, but with a cold-sweat realization it became apparent that we were out of our depth.

I could feel a bit of pushback. It reminded me of the time I left the air-conditioned Benito Juárez International Airport into the sweltering heat of Mexico City. It was like walking into a wall; I almost scurried back into the airport. But I did the same as I did then and just pushed through it. Joey wasn't doing so well. She was pale and sweating. She looked awful. I did pause and wonder if we should take five minutes, but then I thought again about all the exposure this would get us. Getting to the bottom of this wouldn't just get us viral, it'd make our profile go *stratospheric*. Maybe we could get our own network show. I'd been thinking about it for a while; I even had a title: *Secrets of Spirits Unlimited*—I could see that on Netflix. I just needed a big juicy case to hang the pitch on. And it doesn't get much bigger or juicier than incidents on the "discovered" floor at the Cruthers, and the Dark Orchid. We didn't even need any hard proof. Some wobbly, blurry footage, and conjecture from, maybe, a hotel employee saying "I never liked going to that floor," or "I once saw a lady who I think was a ghost." That kind of nonsense. And there's a bit of a buzz about the Dark Orchid at the moment.. I'd asked Joey to make up some shit about picking up whispers from her ghost saying that she "demands her killer be brought to justice" or some other kind of vague nonsense, but she stubbornly refused to play ball. I was sure I could convince her; it didn't have to be a big production number. I'd even been in touch with some producers who were pretty excited. This could finally have been the making of me—the making of *us*.

I'd barely set foot on floor six and a half when I had to duck as a chair shot toward my head and smashed into pieces on the wall behind me.

"What the fuck!" I bunched my fists ready for the motherfucker that threw the chair at me, but it was like we'd walked into a storm. Pieces of furniture were flying through the air. Joey and I dodged the debris. There was the sound of taunting laughter all around us, and splinters of furniture and shards of glass and mirror whirled around the space. I could also detect the strong smell of burned toast in the air. My anger quickly turned to fear. An unseen force was causing this chaos. My fight turned to flight. I turned around to get out but the door was stuck behind us. The number of objects flying toward us increased, including parts of tables.

Joey and I shielded our heads with our arms and ran further in. The chaos increased when we got down some corridors and decreased down others. Too late, I realized that we were mice in a maze and that we were being pushed where the unseen force wanted us to go, until we found ourselves in the eye of the storm.

We were facing a stained-glass window, but it was like no window I'd ever seen. I heard voices. A strained voice with an

Eastern European accent called out, "Milán! Milán!" The person sounded like they were in pain. I looked around to try and find the place where the voice was coming from; one moment it was surrounding me, but then then it was gone. I saw a flash of a smiling bald man with a gold tooth, leering at me.

"Gentlemen, shall we put the knives away?" he said with a Brazilian accent and lunged at me.

I fell back, but he disappeared. I felt faint, as if life was being sucked from me. I looked down and there were vines, roots, and branches circling themselves around me, piercing my clothes and skin. I fought, to get myself free, but the more I fought the more enmeshed I became.

Looming over me was an ash-gray tree, which was moving closer. I thrashed about and suddenly found myself back in the corridor, as though nothing had happened. I laughed, either because I didn't believe what'd just happened or didn't know what else to do. Joey looked terrified. Then I saw what she was looking at. We were still in the corridor, but we'd been transported through time and a woman I recognized as the Dark Orchid was backing away from someone I didn't. We could see the events unfolding but couldn't hear anything. Everything was opaque, like there was an extra layer of time being put on top of ours. I felt like I was frozen to the spot. I looked over at Joey, whose eyes remained wide open in alarm. As we watched this record of the past, a ribbon of energy sparked out of the window and started dragging the Dark Orchid toward it. She struggled and let out a silent scream as the energy ribbon began to cut through her at her midriff, at which point, like a popped soap bubble, the vision disappeared.

"We've got to get the fuck away from here!"

"I've—" Joey was stopped as a vortex opened up around us. In the middle of the swirling energy, like a spider in a web, was what looked like a human–goat chimera. The vortex turned from purple to crimson and slowly disappeared to leave us standing in the hotel corridor, facing the window.

I'm sure I heard someone drop something a floor above us, but there is no floor there, just the roof. And I heard someone cough...

It was as if a storm had passed.

I laughed. "Maybe we're—"

The corridor was suddenly bathed in a sickly, piss-yellow light and I felt myself being pulled toward the window. I could see the same happening to Joey. We must have gotten too close. This was what it must be like in a tar pit, getting sucked down. The window was pulsating, and we couldn't get away. I looked across at Joey and could see the corridor through her; she was becoming transparent; fading away! I looked down at my hand and the same thing was happening to me. I could see something through the window... There was a flash, and I saw that we were in a forest.

Before I could adjust to where we were, something came crashing through the forest, tearing trees from the ground and throwing them aside. I fell and saw the creature bearing down on me. Patches of fur were missing, revealing scars and scabbed-over cuts. It was missing half of one of its horns. It has red scar in the shape of a pentangle on its forehead, and two faces mashed into one, snarling and conflicting, with three baleful eyes looking out.

It scooped up a screaming Joey and galloped off with her. I scrambled to my feet but, as I tried to run after it, I felt something wrapping itself around my legs and then my arms. The more I struggled, the tighter it became, and I drifted into a fog.

*

I don't know how long I've been here. Days? Weeks? Time has no dominion in this realm. This place wraps itself around you like a damp blanket. The first thing I became aware of was Phantoms Inc. turning up.

If I had the energy, I'd be scared for them. I know in the pit of my stomach that none of us will leave this sick, damned place. None of us.

CHAPTER NINETEEN

Marshall

I'm the first to spot the blood-red stone.

"We must be on the right path" I say, and before too long we're in front of another part of the forest depicted in the window: a cave with a red ring around the entrance.

"Do you wanna go in?" Conner asks.

"Do you?"

"No."

"Shall we go in anyway?"

"No."

I get behind Conner and begin to push.

"Ahhh, stop it!"

The cave is chilly. Not cool like some caves. *Chilly*. And the walls look weird. They have an odd shine. Reluctantly I reach out and touch one. In common with the impossible room back in the hotel, it has a horrible organic feel about it, as though we're not really in a cave at all, but in the throat of some huge beast.

"So do you think this will lead to the castle?" Conner asks.

"It would seem to make sense. It's the next panel in the window, so it's a natural progression." As I'm talking my feet touch something. I hope it's nothing small, furry, and squeaky. I sneak a look and what I can see in the gloom looks like dirty, gnarled bones. God, I hope they're animal bones. I decide not to tell Conner. He doesn't need to be more anxious. You don't have to be psychic to pick up on his nerves. He's chewing his lip and absentmindedly tapping his pocket for his antacids.

We gradually make our way through the cave but we literally can't see the light at the end of the tunnel. And now Conner's thumb is starting to twitch. Time for some distraction.

"Do you think Joey will be pleased to see us?"

"Is she ever?"

We both laugh.

"But really, you've been getting help messages from her so surely, she'll be pleased to see us? She wanted us to find the centerpiece. And that's what we did."

"Dunno." He shrugs. "You'd think so, but there was something *off* about the messages."

"Off in what way?"

"Dunno." He shrugs again. "Just *off*. She's never asked me for help before."

"She's never been trapped in an occult realm before."

"True dat."

He shoves his hands deep into his pockets, which is an indication that the conversation is over. Boy, he can hold a grudge when he wants. We trudge along until we come to a dead end. In front of us is a rock face.

"Oh great. So we did this for nothing? But to be fair it's been a lot of laughs; we should walk into cold, dark caves more often."

"No, look!" Conner points at the rock.

"What? I—"

Something begins to glow. In a circle is what, at first, looks like just a random collection of shapes, but which are annoyingly familiar…

I remember where I know them from. "It's the runes around the window!"

Conner nods. "But they're in a different order here. Hold on, I've got an idea." And he begins tentatively touching the runes. He does it in a very specific order, hesitating over some, and being more decisive with others. "I'm following the order that they're on the window."

Each rune glows red as Conner touches it. As he progresses, the glow becomes brighter and his smile grows wider.

"Yes! Yes! I think I've got it!"

Before our eyes the rock face becomes opaque and the fucked-up melty chocolate castle swims into view. Conner presses the last rune and then puts his hand on the surface, which has become a membrane, and presses his palm into it.

"We just need to push through!" Conner says, laughing, and I join him to try and get through to the castle. The former rock face is very pliable and soft; it feels like only one last effort will get us through.

"Conner?" says an ethereal voice.

"Joey! We're coming!" yells Conner.

But I'm not sure it's her.

It feels like the membrane is just about to give way when we literally get some pushback. An invisible force knocks me off my feet, sending me skidding in the dirt. Conner has managed to stay upright. Both of his palms are outstretched, and he's been pushed back from the membrane. He's trying to get back to it but he's like a man walking against a storm.

"If I can just…" His teeth are gritted, and sweat is dripping off him, but I think he'll be able to—

The next thing I know we're tumbling across the ground. The cave has spewed us out back into the forest. After we've stopped rolling we end up, again, in an undignified heap.

"Stop it!" Conner says—like it was a choice of mine—as we untangle ourselves from each other.

"Well that went well," I say as I dust myself off.

"I'm not strong enough." Conner buries his head in his hands.

"What do we—"

Out of the foliage walks a bewildered, good-looking man. He's got short curly hair and a thin old-school mustache and has soot over his face as though he's been near something that has blown up. Lines of sweat streak the soot.

God, his face is so familiar, but my head is still a bit foggy from our transportation through to this realm. This is really going to bug me; I should know his face.

He's wearing what would be a smart blazer, white shirt, and slacks. Smart if there weren't burn marks on the blaze still letting off wisps of smoke, burn holes in the shirt, and soot on the slacks. He seems as surprised to see us as we are to see him. He casually pats his blazer to try and put out the last of the embers. It's only then that he seems to notice his surroundings.

"Where the devil am I? And who the devil are you two?" But he flashes us a smile as though he's just walked into a bar.

"We were going to ask you the same question."

"The last thing I remember is being in my lab. I was experimenting with something, something very exciting and very important…" He looks lost then snaps back. "…Anyway, yes, there was a bright light—a flash—and then I was here."

He looks around while he pats his hair into place and smooths the creases out in his pants. He's sweating profusely.

"Where the hell is here?"

"We don't know. We just got here ourselves."

"My name's Jack, by the way." He thrusts his hand out. He's got a firm handshake and looks me square in the eyes and smiles, his eyes darting back and forth as though he's trying to find out what I'm thinking.

"I'm Marshall, and this is Conner."

He shakes Conner's hand, which makes him wince.

"We've got to find a way out of here."

"Why?" Jacks asks with a smile on his lips and a twinkle in his eye. "We've found our way into an unearthly realm. This is a once in a lifetime opportunity to explore! Who knows what pearls of esoteric knowledge we will be party to? Knowledge! Forbidden knowledge perhaps?" He nudges me in my side with his elbow, and winks.

I laugh nervously even though I have no idea what he's going on about. "You don't understand, Jack; there are creatures in the forest—horrible creatures!"

"Fantastic!"

That is not the reaction I was anticipating.

"We need to discover what these creatures are!"

"No, we don't! We need to run away from them!"

A noise like the tearing of a chicken carcass echoes around the forest, and this is followed by a tremble. The ground rattles.

Conner, Jack, and I try—unsuccessfully—to stay on our feet when a huge ridge pitches up in front of us and a monstrous bellow echoes around the forest. It feels like this world is tearing itself apart.

The terrain seems to have a mind of its own. Roaring and screaming, pieces of it rear up and parts of it drop down into mini ravines, sending clouds of dirt up into the air to rain down on us. It's like being in a not-particularly-fun house as the ground shifts and pitches us about. I manage to get to my feet for around five seconds; after that I just cling on for dear life.

Eventually, after what seems like an age, things settle down and I look around. I'm relieved to see Conner getting unsteadily to his feet and dusting himself off.

"Where's Jack?" I shout.

Conner looks around and shrugs. "Haven't seen him, but we've got to find Joey."

He's not wrong, but I can't help looking behind me. I start thinking.

"Yeah, we'll find Joey, but we've got to find our bearings." In a flash I realize where I know Jack from. Of course! "Wait! Jack. Could he have been…?"

There's a loud bang as one of the mangled trees falls over. I don't wait for Conner to take the lead this time; I run off and he follows me. This turns out to be a terrible mistake because, nearly too late, I realize that I'm running out of ground and I'm looking at a cliff edge. I stop just in time.

"Thank God for tha—"

Conner barrels into the back of me and we both go tumbling over the edge into darkness.

As we fall, I try to clutch onto something. More by luck than judgment I manage to slow my descent, but only slightly. Conner must have done the same because we land together, in an undignified heap at the bottom. We get up and, apart from a few scrapes, we're both okay—which is a bit of a miracle, to be honest, 'cause it was a pretty steep fall. As we're dusting ourselves off—again—it seems that somebody wasn't as lucky as us. In front of us, face down in the dirt, is a body.

CHAPTER TWENTY

Marshall

Conner nudges the body with his foot.

"Don't do that!"

Conner shrugs.

"Well, we don't know…" I carefully roll him over and he's still breathing. He's a burly-looking guy wearing scuffed, dirty overalls. He's largely bald with scrubby stubble, which is just a day or two away from being an actual beard. He looks familiar as his eyes flutter open.

"Oh, thank God!" He's got a thick New York accent and the penny drops that he's one of the workmen we saw on Eugene's phone: one of the men who disappeared.

We help him sit up and look around.

As he becomes aware of his surroundings, his face drops. "Ah Jesus, I was hoping I was concussed or something. But nah, I'm still here."

"How did you get here?" I ask.

"Same way as you, I suspect. The window. I'm Sam."

We nod a greeting.

He wipes a hand over his face. "This place is fucked up! Terrible, horrible!"

"Yeah, we worked that out. What happened to your friend?"

"My friend?"

"The other workman?"

He looks around. "Rod? He was just with me…"

"Did you just wake up here?" I ask.

"No, we've been walking around here for…" He wipes his hand over his face again. "Shit, I don't know if it's hours or days. Time is a bit fucked-up here."

"We're starting to get that impression," agrees Conner. "What have you discovered in the forest?"

"Apart from it's fucked-up? Well, one minute we were in the Cruthers and the next we were here. This place feels ill. We tried to find a way outta here."

"And how did that go?"

"Yeah, not so good." He gives me a withering look and then continues. "You know, I didn't sign up for this shit. We thought we could hear a girl's voice coming from a cave, but we didn't stick around. We were freaked out as it was."

"That's where we need to be. Could you take us back there?"

He pulls a face and rubs the back of his neck. "I'm not keen. I still dunno what's happened to Rod."

"Don't you—"

"Look, fellas, I'd love to help but—"

"Her name is Joey," Conner blurts out.

"What?"

"The girl you heard is called Joey…"

"Probably," I hope he doesn't hear me mutter.

"…and she may be the key to getting us out of here. We can protect you."

That's a very bold claim from Conner. Sam looks at me and I just nod my agreement.

"Okay then, I'll help you. I think I know the way. We need to keep a look out for a blood-red stone. It's very distinctive."

"We've seen it!"

"Yeah, and it's one of the only things that doesn't seem to change location in relation to the cave. Once we find that we hang a right. That's another fucked-up thing about this screwy place: just when you think you've got it worked out, it goes all screwy again."

"What, like the geography changes? Suddenly somewhere that was five minutes away is an hour away?"

"Yeah! There's normally a tearing sound and then everything changes. That's when I must have lost Rod. We should be okay for a while now, but we'd better get going before it happens again."

Sam leads the way. We follow him into a clearing and down a twisting path.

"That's another thing I've noticed about this place: there ain't no birds—well, not as we know them. I ain't seen no birds and I ain't *heard* no birds."

"We've heard…noises," says Conner. "There are some animals in the forest?"

"Oh yes," Sam says with a humorless chuckle. "There are *animals* in the forest."

Which kills the conversation stone dead for a couple of minutes, until we find the stone again. This time it's next to an ash-gray tree, which looks like it may be dead.

"There you go!" says Sam.

"Brilliant!" says Conner.

I think he's being a bit over-enthusiastic, to be honest.

"Right, so—"

A branch from the tree whips around Sam's neck.

We rush to help him, but, like the tree holding Davey, when we try and get our fingers underneath to try and loosen its grip, it only tightens. It's joined by another branch, which lifts Sam off his feet.

"Helllll!" he screeches.

He's desperately clutching at his neck as another branch shoots out and pierces just under his hand causing a fountain of blood to spurt out. He thrashes about in the clutches of the tree. His blood splashes onto the bark, which instantly revives it. The bark that was previously an ash-gray color now bristles with a red vigor. A hideous shiver runs through the trunk of the tree as though it's quivering in delight. Tendrils snake out toward us.

"Fuck!"

I run off, and of course Conner is already way ahead of me,

but I'm scared shitless so I quickly catch up with him, nearly tripping over the uneven ground.

When we've run far enough away—hopefully—I turn to Conner and say:

"Jesus Christ! What was that?"

"A vampire tree!" Conner says, also managing to laugh and cry at the same time. "We said we'd protect him."

"No, *you* said you'd protect him," I say, too harshly. Shit! Conner looks crushed. "Sorry, didn't mean that. There was nothing we could do, after all. Fucking vampire trees…"

"Suppose so."

"This is going to sound cold, but we need to get going and find Joey, otherwise Sam's death will mean nothing."

He nods, but I can tell he's not happy.

"I think when we were up by the—fucking hell—vampire tree, I saw another approach. If we circle around we can avoid the…you-know-what…"

Conner nods again, and we set off, this time in silence and keeping as much distance as we can between us and the trees.

We find the blood-red stone, but this time we're the other side of it, and, rather worryingly, the vampire tree has disappeared. Fuck. Is it roaming around stalking us? Getting taken out by a vampire tree would be a really shit way to go.

"Which way did Sam say to go?" I ask.

"He said hang a right."

"Okay, so we're the opposite side, so that means we hang a left?"

"Yeah, sounds good to me."

We look around and there are no obvious landmarks; it's the same sick forest.

"Marshall! Marshall! The trees are looking at me in a weird way!"

It's not like that time that we *accidentally* ate those brownies that Marv got from his friend in the village; the trees do seem to be swaying in our direction and definitely are looking at us in a weird way.

"Let's just back away slowly…"

But, of course, Conner has run off like a headless chicken. This time he doesn't get very far because he almost runs straight into a thicket of razor-sharp brambles, which definitely weren't there a few moments ago. And the trees are creeping in on us. Yeah, this *is* like the time we ate those brownies, but no way near as much fun.

I look around for any gaps, any escape route. Maybe if I wrap my jacket around my arms, I could charge the newly arrived brambles and get through?

Conner clearly reads my mind; he's good at that. "Don't! It'll rip you apart."

The forest seems to be savoring its approach.

There's a rustle, which gets steadily louder. At first I think I'm imagining it, but a small opening appears in the brambles and rays of purple light shine out through gaps, like spotlights. The purple light beams become thicker and force open a bigger gap in the brambles. We can see a clear corridor through them, and at the end of it stands a woman with jet-black hair and brown eyes, with a purple shimmer around her. We don't hesitate and run toward freedom. The brambles cut me as I run past, slicing into my jeans. I sense that the foliage is bristling to crash back in on us, but with some relief we tumble into a clearing at the foot of the woman, who has a ghost of a smile on her lips. She throws her hair back in a long-practiced—but nevertheless beguiling—move.

"Hello, boys."

"You've got to be fucking joking." I instantly know who she is.

"You'll have to forgive me; I haven't seen anyone for a while."

"Are you…?"

"My name is Mary-Jane Mountmore, and I'm here to help."

CHAPTER TWENTY-ONE

"**R**rright." Conner narrows his eyes at our new, unlikely savior.

"You have to be on your guard constantly in this place; it doesn't conform to the natural way of things. The forest has its own screwy rules, and—this is gonna sound kooky—be careful around the trees!"

"Oh, we've learned that lesson," I reply. "Uhhh…so you're Mary-Jane Mountmore?"

"Yes, but please call me May."

"You're an actress?"

"Yes."

"It's just that we…" Unlike Conner, I don't have much experience of talking to dead people. "…weren't expecting to… errr…meet you. I'm Marshall Thompson."

"And I'm Conner Deal."

"And we're Phantoms Inc.!"

Mary-Jane—May—laughs. "Oh, I'm so sorry! I didn't mean to…Of course, you're Phantoms Inc."

"Don't worry, we get that a lot."

"You've come here from the Cruthers Hotel, haven't you?" she asks.

"Yeah, we sorta got cornered."

"The Infidels?"

"Yeah, but I suspect our experience of the Infidels is very different from yours."

"How did you get here?" I ask.

The brassy confidence that she's displayed until now slips.

"I don't quite know." She looks around, almost as though she's seeing the forest for the first time. "It's so hazy, like I'm in a dream. One moment I was backed into a corner up on that strange floor in the hotel, and the next moment I was here. I don't know how long it's been. I might have been here for hours, or I might have been here for years. Time is like syrup here: sludgy and hard to get through."

"What can you tell us about this place?"

She perks up. "The geography here isn't fixed; it shifts roughly every four hours. I try to keep track of time and place, but it's so difficult."

"We've found out. We need to get to the castle. We tried to get to it through the cave but—"

"It threw you out?" she asks.

We nod vigorously.

"You're lucky to have got away with that."

"Didn't feel lucky at the time," I say.

"You're not the first people to try to get through to the castle. Trust me, you're lucky it just threw you out."

I decide not to pursue that any further.

"I'll help you to get to the castle," May says.

"But what if—?"

"I think together we can do it."

"I dunno," says Conner. "We got pretty badly scuffed up trying to get through last time. Isn't there another way to the castle?"

"No. Trust me, I've tried. I can get you through the cave. But if I help you, you have to help me. The Infidels are trying to bring the Cruthers—or the creature they have become—back into our world. We have to ensure that it can never get back to our world, because if it does…"

She leaves that hanging in the air.

"At least they don't have the centerpiece." She chuckles. "I hid it right under their nos—" She sees the look on our faces. "What?"

"Errr…"

"The thing is…"

"Oh no, don't tell me you…"

"'Fraid so. Isn't that how we got here?"

She runs a hand over her face and little sparks of purple twinkle.

"That makes it more important than ever to stop the creature. It's been looking for a way out."

"I thought the window was the only way in and out."

"So did I, but I've seen others here from our world. They've come and gone, so there must be other ways to get here. The creature knows that too, but now you've given them the best chance to get out of here."

"Sorry." It doesn't seem quite adequate, somehow.

"But the message I got from Joey said we needed the centerpiece. I couldn't ignore that," sulks Conner.

"Why haven't you tried to get out?" I ask, attempting to change the subject.

"I don't think I can. I'm here, but I'm not…I think I'm bound to this place. Even when I think about getting back to our world there seems to be some kind of block on it. I don't know what happened to me on the other side."

She looks at us and we shift uneasily on our feet. Conner stares at his trainers and I turn my attention to the sky. When we look back at May, she's studying our faces.

"Yes, I thought so," she says with a sigh. "My glimmer has gotten brighter since I got here. I know you've got it too, Conner. I can feel it. But maybe it's not strong enough for you to get through to the castle on your own. That's good, though. It means you have something to get back to in our world."

Does he blush? I half expect him to say "Ahhh, shucks."

"The creature wants to use my power to break through to

our world, but together we can use our powers to defeat it. I can't do it alone. I've had battles with the creature, and I've barely been able to hold my own. It's getting stronger. I worry that the next time we fight, I'll lose, so I've been hiding. You can hear the creature coming a mile off, so that hasn't been too difficult. Let's work together."

"But what about Joey? We have to rescue her. She's in the castle," says Conner, a bit too quickly.

"Fine, fine, we have to rescue Joey from the castle. How do you guys feel like being knights in shining armor?"

We both shrug. I can't honestly see Joey being comfortable in the role of damsel in distress. We look at each other. Neither of us want to go back to the cave after last time.

"The thing is—"

May pushes me from behind. She's surprisingly strong. We seem to be getting pushed around a lot since we landed here.

"Come on, you two. We've got to go."

The Dark Orchid—sorry, *May*—leads us on a surprisingly quiet trek through the forest.

The silence is broken by Conner. "When you said we weren't the first people to try and get to the castle…"

Oh great, Conner, you had to go and ask.

"Yes, I've seen travelers of the hidden realms find their way here. They already know that it's a place of great power, but they quickly realize that it's also a place of great danger, and evil and they try to get back out. Very few manage to get out."

"What happens to the ones that don't?"

May stops dead and looks at Conner. "Very few manage to get out," she says slowly.

"Oh." The penny drops.

"But we're going to be fine. I can feel it." She throws a mock punch at Conner's shoulder, which actually does land.

"Ow!"

"I hardly touched you!"

"That's his bad shoulder." Actually I think it might be his other one, but Conner's hypochondria is a movable feast.

"Sheesh!"

She walks on at a pace. Even though I've been running a lot recently, I find it difficult to keep up with May; I think it's because of how irregular the terrain is, and to be honest how *hostile* it is. I pass close to something that looks like a brambly type of weed and it actually *snaps* at me. Like an over-excited dog! I let out a high-pitched yelp when I avoid the dog-plant, which gets a smirk from May. Meanwhile, she's negotiating her way through the forest like it's second nature to her. Can't say the route looks familiar to me. It doesn't seem the same way we came the last time, but that would chime with what we keep hearing about the fluid nature of the geography.

The three of us stand in front of the cave and I can almost feel Conner wobbling beside me. I glance to my side and, sure enough, he's chewing his lip and his right leg is doing a bit of an Elvis swivel. The opening of the cave looks even *more* like the mouth of a gigantic animal. I really don't want to go back in there.

"See, boys, it ain't so bad!" says May.

"Are you fucking joking?"

I wonder if she's looking at the same cave as me. Right on cue the sound of tearing chicken rolls across the forest and a mournful sigh, which then descends into a growl, comes out from the cave.

Now Conner's *left* leg has joined the swivel.

I clear my throat. "I'd that suggest that—"

May pushes past us, rolls her eyes, and strides into the tar black entrance of the cave. I squeeze what I hope is Conner's good shoulder—it's hard to tell anymore—and we follow her in.

"Now, I can help you through the cave. We've—I've—tried it before, although there's sorta never really been a reason for me to go all the way through to the castle."

We've tried it before?

"Rrright." Conner says and he's doing that squinty eye thing at her again.

"Tell me again what happened when you got to the rock face," she says, changing the subject. And it works with Conner, 'cause he suddenly snaps to attention.

"Oh! Oh! It was really weird."

"Right, like there's anything normal in this place!"

"Ha! Yeah, you're right! But what was weird about this was that the rock face changed to being kinda…"

"Spongy?"

"Yes!" Conner says pointing at May.

Honestly, I don't know what's up with him. One minute he's

all doubtful and *"Rrright"* and the next he's like a little puppy with her. I don't get it.

*

Conner

I don't trust her.

Yeah, she's got the glimmer, but she's hiding something. But…but I can't help myself getting a little stupid around her. When May talks to me I can hear my heartbeat, I can feel myself begin to heat up, and the hairs on my arm stand up. It's a bit like when I'm channeling a spirit, but I don't have that horrible feeling in my teeth. I can't help but think that having these feelings about someone who is supposed to have died over half a century ago is inappropriate. I don't think there's a handbook for this. I'd love to say that I'm being all giggly and bouncy so that I can find out what she's up to, but no, she just makes me giggly and bouncy.

She leads and we follow down the cave until we get to the rock face. I can see the dents where Marshall landed and the drag marks where I was pushed back. I put my palm on the rock. Hard to believe that it is anything other than rock, solid and cold.

"What did you do?"

"I thought you'd done this before."

"I have," she says quickly. "It's just been a long time. I forget exactly—"

"Exactly in which order to touch the runes?"

"Yes!"

"Hmmm. Okay, well, uh, it's lucky that I do."

Am I a little too eager to please? Maybe, but I start tracing my fingers around the runes scratched into the rock. As before, they glow red and become more intense as I touch each in the order that I remember from the window. The rock face becomes pliable again and my palm begins to push into it.

"It's happening again!" I shout.

Just as before, the image of the castle swims into view. It's so close I can almost touch it.

"Help me!" a voice pleads from the other side.

"Joey?"

I'm so near!

Then—as before—I feel the pushback. The membrane and castle are receding, falling through my fingers. I can't hold out for long.

"I need help!" I shout, and immediately May is by my side.

She puts both palms out in front of her. A purple halo fizzes around her and tendrils of purple energy crackle from her fingers—sorta like the emperor in *Return of the Jedi*, but that's not an important detail. I can feel the pushback begin to weaken, but it's still like walking in treacle. Gradually it gets easier and the image of the castle solidifies, and we're almost there.

"Marshall! We're going through!" I yell as we start to push.

We're walking into the membrane of the rock face. It's pretty disgusting, like flailing around in warm jelly—which ain't as much fun as it sounds. I look behind me and Marshall has an expression on his face like he's stepped in something on the sidewalk.

We seem to have been wading through this amniotic soup for an eternity but, like breaking the surface of the sea after a deep dive—or so I've been told—we're suddenly spluttering into the other side. Despite what it felt like coming through here, my clothes are bone dry, and the same would seem to be true of the other two, looking at them.

When we've recovered from our trip, we stand and stare at the castle

"I can't believe…" starts May. "I mean this is the first time I've ever managed to get through! Amazing!" She hugs me and a little thrill runs through my body, like I used to get around Joey. Not that we ever hugged, of course.

"What now?" asks Marshall. He sounds pissed off. He's probably just jealous that May hugged me and not him.

"I suppose we go in?" I say but having made the suggestion I'm not keen. If anything the castle is even *less* inviting than the cave was. I feel my stomach ulcer acting up.

"Go on, then." says Marshall.

"Well I…"

But May has rushed ahead of us and is bounding up what passes for stairs towards the castle.

"Come on, slugabeds!" she calls back.

For one, I don't know what a slugabed is supposed to be, and for a second, I have a nagging doubt about following her. But Marshall walks after her.

"Maybe it's better if I stay outside and keep guard, 'cause—"

I hear a growling noise and change my mind.

The entrance to the castle has two large pillars each side, which shoot off into the stratosphere. We're standing in a large, empty space and ahead of us is a rough approximation of a huge staircase. I say approximation because, like everything about this castle, it sorta looks like it was grown rather than built. Nothing in the building has a sharp edge: it's all bumpy, organic, and wrinkled. The floor is uneven but not as irregular as the terrain outside. Some of the craggy ground has been flattened out and even has a bit of a shine to it, but this still doesn't detract from the essential *wrongness* of the place. It's almost like a child's drawing after a visit to a castle, if that child was seeing a medical professional. The light has that same *sick* feeling about it as outside, but in here it's full of dust.

Something other than the dust is irritating me, though. This place seems familiar…

"It's the Cruthers Hotel!" Marshall laughs as he says it.

He's right!

"A fucked-up version, but still the Cruthers Hotel!"

He's right about that as well. It's an attempt to recreate the Cruthers, but it's way off. For example, what would be one of the enclaves in the actual hotel, here looks like someone has taken a chunk of earth out of the side of a mountain in preparation to do more work. And looking at the hollow there's something else in there, something embedded. A rock maybe?

"What's in that space at the actual hotel?" I ask, nodding toward the hollow.

"The brothers Cruthers."

"Oh yeah! It's that creepy portrait of the brothers that…"

Marshall is pointing. He manages a croak. "No, the brothers…" All the emotion has drained from his voice.

I see why.

Standing in front of the space, as though they'd just materialized, are two men: one is a slim, dapper dressed in a smart suit; the other is a taller, heavier set with a scar across his face. Total opposites, but they share the same eyes. They are the portrait brought to life.

I edge backward. At least I try to edge backward, but find I'm rooted to the spot, and so is Marshall. There is a purple light dancing about us.

"I've brought you what you wanted," says May, addressing the brothers.

"Ahhh, fuck." I hear Marshall say.

As I'm literally swept off my feet, I'm sure I hear someone else speak, but I'm taken away too quickly to catch what is said

*

Mary-Jane

What have I done? How did I get to be like this? If only I had never met Miles…

*

We were together in the room. The others were taking a break and Miles began to read the incantations. I'd heard them so often that I began to chant them along with him.

Instantly things changed: the light in the room changed to a purple hue, and it felt like there was a sticky, static energy in the room.

"You must never, *never* read the incantations out at the same time as me."

I giggled and aped his "never, *never*", but stopped when I saw he looked genuinely scared.

"It will unleash a force that not even the strongest esoteric practitioner can control."

"Fine, I understand."

But he remained pensive for the next few moments.

At first, I thought Miles's talk of rituals and spells was all some kind of hokey Halloween nonsense just to impress me, but it soon dawned on me that he meant it all and that it was serious. In a similar way, his questions about my grandfather's time in New York had become more than just friendly chat, and then he was putting pressure on me to investigate what my grandfather might have left out here—I mean he was *really* putting the pressure on me. But I was intrigued and I felt a desire to seek out what my grandfather stored away. It was like an inexplicable force drawing me in.

Which all led me to the docks on a suitably foggy evening. I met an old nightwatchman. He checked my ID, nodded as though he wasn't particularly interested, and I followed him to a small, run-down warehouse. It was hard to believe that anything of any worth or importance could be stored within. The nightwatchman unlocked the door and walked off; obviously he, too, thought there was nothing of worth in there.

I entered the warehouse. Inside it was immaculate, not even any dust. The whole place was empty except for just one thing, which I sensed more than saw. Propped up against the far end of the space was something circular covered in a red sheet. I don't know why but I felt a stab of anxiety about approaching the object. My hand trembled as I pulled the sheet away.

It felt like removing the sheet had removed some kind of protection. A circular stained-glass panel was revealed, with the image of a leering satanic goat with a pentangle on its forehead. The Baphomet centerpiece, I'd seen drawings of it at the meetings.

"Oh God, what have I done?"

I sensed I was being watched, and not just by the picture of the goat, but by who or what? Of course, I already knew. That's when I tried to run.

I tried.

I left the warehouse. The nightwatchman was standing like he'd been frozen to the spot, his eyes and mouth wide open in a rictus of shock. I checked for a pulse, which wasn't there. With the stained-glass panel under my arm I thought about my next move.

Where could I go?

Which was when the storm began to swirl around me. I

brought the glass up to protect me from a sudden onslaught of rain. I didn't know where I was going, I just knew I had to get out of the storm. I looked up to get my bearings. I was at O'Brien Avenue. The storm grew more ferocious as I ran, and then it occurred to me where I could seek sanctuary. Gold kept an apartment just a few blocks away; I could hole up there until the storm blew over. I could catch up on all his bitchy gossip—who was screwing who and why—all with a warming glass of something. Glass panel in front of me I headed down an alley, but there was an almighty bang and just yards away from me a lamppost crashed to the ground, sparks flying, and blocked my way. I skidded to a halt, turned around, and headed back.

Where else could I go?

"Mary-Jane?" A sing-song voice echoed down the street.

I knew it was the Infidels.

They were after me.

Like a mouse in a maze I ran and ducked down the streets and alleyways. As soon as I thought of where I could go, an obstacle presented itself: a car broke down, a tree fell, I pleaded to strangers to help me but it was like they couldn't even see me. I was pushed left and right, around and around, until I was looking up at the imposing visage of the Cruthers Hotel.

Somehow I always knew it would end here.

This was the last place I wanted to be.

I looked at the door. Was there any way I could avoid going in?

"MARY-JANE!"

My head whipped around. I couldn't tell where the voice was coming from so pushed through the doors straight into the lion's den.

Was there anywhere I could hide?

Then—thank God—I saw a friendly face: Henry. Bless him, he was a good kid; he reminded me of my younger brother.

"May!" he said, approaching me like an over-eager dog.

"You've got to get out of here, Henry."

"Why, what's happening? What's that?" he asked, gesturing to the centerpiece.

"That's why you've got to get out of here. There are some people coming to try and get this, and they can't have it."

"I can help!"

Ah, bless! Then it suddenly dawned on me what I could do.

"Henry, in a few minutes there's going to be men coming through that door; you've got to buy me some time. I'm going to hide this. They'll never guess. Distract them. When I don't have to worry about this, I can come up with a better plan. Thanks, Henry."

Having hidden the centerpiece, it was me that was playing hide 'n' seek. I was right up as far as I could go in the hotel. I turned a corner and there he was: Miles. His hands were outstretched; one of his palms was moving clockwise and the other counterclockwise, and there was the crackle of energy between them.

"Where's the centerpiece, Mary-Jane?"

"Yeah, like I'm gonna—"

He unleashed a bolt of energy toward me. I got ready for it to hit, instinctively put my hands up, and found, to my amazement, that it stalled in my hands. Miles was as angry as I was surprised and his palms started moving faster, which made me giggle. He sent more bolts out and I stopped all of them. He was right: I do have the glimmer.

Then he began to push back with a ferocity and anger that I couldn't handle. He was snarling like a wild animal, saliva flying, teeth bared, and I couldn't fight it. He maneuvered me past the window and the energy bolts pushed me up against a wall. I felt the crunch of the masonry against my back and shards of pain leaped up to my head. As Miles got closer, I could feel a magnetic pull; I was being dragged toward the window. I didn't know if it was because of the pain but I could feel myself floating. I could see my body below me! I looked dazed, and Miles was watching me. I felt oddly detached from my impending death.

*

After that, I saw the darkness.

CHAPTER TWENTY-TWO

Fucksticks! Why do we always fall for this? I know Conner wasn't sure about the Dark Orchid, but then he went all puppy dog over her.

"At least we've found Joey," Conner says looking at his sneakers and refusing to look me in the eye.

We have indeed. We've been locked in a room with Joey Santiago, one half of Spirits Unlimited—possibly the only business on the planet with a stupider name than ours. Joey is around five foot six with long brown hair, brown eyes, a complexion from her Mexican ancestry, and right now she looks pissed off. Her bushy eyebrows are furrowed.

"Some rescue this is. She played you for the idiots you are."

"Thanks, that *really* helps," I bat back.

She sighs, stands up, and kicks the door, which remains

resolutely locked. "Tell me again what happened."

"Why, it won't change anything." This is a fucking horrible room, and I've been locked in some truly horrible rooms. Everything is sticky.

"Okay…We got through the membrane in the cave—bop bop bop—then into the castle, we see the gruesome twosome, the Dark Orchid sells us down the river, then get thrown into this delightful room with your happy smiley face. Have I missed anything?" I direct the last sentence at Conner but he's still looking down at his sneakers.

"But why?"

"But why *what*?"

"Why has the Dark Orchid sold you down the river? What does she have to gain?"

"Your guess is as good as mine."

"Maybe she was tricked as well," Conner mutters.

"I doubt it from her 'I brought you what you wanted' comment."

"Well then, did the Cruthers say anything?" Joey asks.

I shake my head. We hardly had enough time to notice 'cause as soon as the Dark Orchid had gone all Lando on us *something* picked us up, dragged us along, and threw our sorry asses in this room.

"They didn't say anything. They just nodded at her, like 'good job well done'," Conner says to his feet.

"Hang on a minute, I thought the creature out there— Captain Goaty—was the Cruthers?" I ask.

"It is."

"So who did we just get ambushed by?"

"That's the brothers Cruthers," answers Joey.

"Right…" I look up at the ceiling, which is made up of some sort of stalactites, which look razor sharp at the tips. They've turned the same color brown that is the main theme of age throughout the castle, tapering into an off-white color. When I realize that the color reminds me of pus I have to stop myself gagging. I bring my mind back to Captain Goaty, the brothers Cruthers, and what Joey just said. I'm getting a headache.

"That makes perfect sense. Not."

"So I'll try and explain this. What you saw earlier is just a projection of the brothers. If you'll excuse my use of the word, what you saw were phantoms. They'd vanish if they tried to leave here. From what I understand, the castle is the beating heart of World Ash; it's been here for as long as World Ash, but like many things in this realm it's malleable. It can change according to the dominant force here. That dominant force, at the moment, is the Cruthers. Faulkmeyer told us a bit about it. I'd expected something nicer. Not sure I fancy immortality here."

"This place existed a long time before the brothers and it will continue a long time after them. I've had a while to do some research. I just have to touch these…" She looks wistfully at the walls. Rather her than me; anytime I've touched anything since we've been here my hand has come away *slimy.* "There's so much history and so many stories coursing through this place, like blood through its veins…"

"Which is all very poetic and *gross*, but did you find out what the gruesome twosome want with us?"

"You're not going to like it." Conner has lost his fascination with his sneakers and is finally looking up.

"When this is over, we're going to seriously look into that pet-finding ability of yours."

Joey raises an eyebrow.

"Go on then, what am I not going to like?"

"Joey, you never sent out an SOS, did you?" Conner asks.

She shakes her head.

"Yeah, it was a trap," he says.

"Why is it always a trap? When will we learn?" When will *Conner* learn?

"Why have they got us her?"

"You're not going to like it," Joey says.

"God, don't you start."

"I think they need me and Conner so that we can use our talents to get them out of this realm and back into ours."

"I notice that Davey and I are not included in that."

Joey and Conner exchange a look.

"Great. Well then, we need to get out of here quick smart."

"No shit, Sherlock," says Joey. "What do you suggest?"

"Right, you said that this place bends to the will of the dominant force?"

She nods.

"Well then, in this room aren't you two Harry Potters the dominant force?"

I half expect to see a light bulb appear over Joey's head, and Conner finally perks up.

"Oi yeah! So…"

I know he doesn't know what to say next and I don't leave him hanging. "So, between the two of you, couldn't you bend our surroundings to your will to conjure up a door? Or open that one?"

Conner looks skeptical until Joey says, "It's worth a go."

"Yeah, go on then. What should we do?"

"Picture the door, but open."

Conner nods.

Joey puts her palms flat and points them at the door.

"Do we have to go full Magneto?" Conner asks.

I can see what he means; the stance is a bit X-Men villain.

"No…" Joey says, "but I find it helps. Gives me a bit of… confidence." She says "confidence" like she's got a marble in her mouth.

Conner shrugs and mirrors her pose. I wonder if scowling, as though they're lifting weights, also helps the process. Despite all their efforts the door remains resolutely shut.

"I don't think—"

"No! Look!" Joey shouts, but at first I don't see anything.

I feel a breeze, which stirs the dust in the room and sends it floating into the light, and then there's a sigh like the sound of autumn leaves rustling in a park, and then—yes! — the door begins to ripple, like someone's thrown a stone into a pond, before it disappears leaving us our escape route.

Joey and Conner are laughing and hugging each other, but as they do there's a shimmering over the doorway, so I grab them and push them through.

We find ourselves in a gnarly, uneven corridor. It looks like every footstep could send you crashing to the floor.

"What do we do now?"

I really wish Conner would stop asking me that.

"Why don't we—"

"Follow me!"

I do as the lady says.

*

Mary-Jane

No one can judge me. I've been tricked and lied to and I'm going to do whatever I have to do to look after myself. I only have myself to rely on and I'm going to do whatever it takes to get back to the other side.

I still don't know what happened to my body in our world after I last saw it, but I know it wasn't good and the look I got from Conner and Marshall seemed to confirm that. When I try to recall what happened before I came over, all I can remember is pain and screaming. If I think about it too much I get a searing headache. But like a sore tooth I keep needling it.

*

I found myself tumbling into a forest clearing after my confrontation with Miles. Smoke was rising from a scorch mark around my waist, the mark looked like it had been left by a belt but I couldn't fathom why. I had an unpleasant copper taste in my mouth like I'd been sucking on a handful of pocket change. The forest was terrifying, with diseased-looking trees and bathed in a sickly yellow light. It felt like a nightmare, but I knew I was awake. I could smell a sweet, rotten smell in the air. I could hear noises floating through the forest—birdsong? It was from no bird I'd ever heard. I felt bruised from my tumble, awake, but in a fog. Within minutes the ground began to shake, which, in turn, shook me into action. I could feel the quake getting closer, and over the treetops I saw a huge, monstrous creature coming toward me. The undergrowth looked sharp and uninviting, but I had no other choice, so stumbled for cover.

As I hid, the vegetation seemed to be actually creeping toward me. Intuitively I held my hand up and saw a crackle of purple energy fizz out and burn it back. I had no time to be surprised as the creature crashed through to the clearing. It was a hideous giant human–goat chimera with three eyes and a red pentangle brand on its forehead. It snorted through its nostrils as it looked around. It seemed to have anticipated that I would be there. It stomped about leaving deep cloven hoof prints in the ground. One of the trees behind the creature moved toward it. Instinctively, almost absentmindedly, the creature swung its knotted, muscle-bound left arm back, shattering the tree's trunk and uprooting the rest of it. The creature gazed around and actually looked in my direction but failed to see me. It stamped one of its hooves down like a toddler in the middle of a tantrum, sending a shockwave through the immediate area, before stomping off, sending trees and plants flying and leaving a cloud of dust in its wake. It had obviously been looking for me.

I should have been seized by fear—and yes, there was a big part of me that wanted to just curl up in a ball and cry—but there was a bigger, fiery part that thought *Godammit! To hell with you! I'm gonna survive!*

My first task was to get my bearings, so I dusted myself off and began to explore.

I discovered that the place has its own rules, but what appeared to be mad at first I now understand has its own logic—a Mad Hatter's logic but still…

Time means nothing here, but I was aware that time had passed: it could've been days; it could've been years. I hadn't felt hungry since arriving, though, which was fortunate as not only was there nothing that looked edible but most of the vegetation actually looked like it could eat you.

Night fell with a carnival of alarming noises, and that is how I found the cave, as somewhere to shelter from the night. The cave was only slightly less terrifying than the rest of the forest. I recognized it as probably the same as the one depicted in the window.

At the end of the cave I came to a rock face. A dead end. But there were inscriptions carved into it in a circle. I traced my finger around the indentations but only saw an effect when I touched the marks in the order I remembered from the window. They glowed red and, as I continued, the rock face began to change. It became malleable and I saw the image of a castle swim into view. Another element from the window.

I knew I had to get to the castle. I pushed myself into what the rock face had become. I didn't get far.

Once, when I was seven years old, I was at the beach with my folks on a sunny day. I was reckless even back then, always pushing to see how far I could go, and on that day I went too far. I waded out in the sea. It looked so welcoming, so calm; the sunlight twinkled on the mottled, foamy waves. I giggled and dove under the sea. My head came up and suddenly the shore seemed miles away and I felt the heckles of panic and tried to swim back, but the harder I swam the farther out I seemed to get and the waves—which at first had been so welcoming—began to pummel me and a current started dragging me under. Twice I was dragged under into the unknowable darkness but managed to fight my way back to the surface, but the third time I lost all my energy and felt a numbing cold. I had begun to black out when I felt a strong arm pull me up. Suddenly I was back, spluttering into the sunlight. My father's strong, hairy, tattooed arm grabbed me up and dragged me out of the sea. Back on the beach there was a lot of shouting and red faces. No ice cream for me that day, but a silent tantrum.

Trying to get to the castle was like that time at the beach: I felt like I'd been shoved, was drowning, and then was suddenly back out and gasping. I don't know how long I'd struggled before it spat me out, skidding along in the dirt. I felt completely drained of energy and I lay where I landed until I could limp to the entrance of the cave like a scolded dog.

I sat in the opening and watched the giant, hoofed legs of the creature stomp past, and prayed that it wouldn't investigate the cave. I didn't have the energy to escape—I felt like a weak newborn ready to be picked off—but thankfully it passed by. *Godammit! To hell with you! I'm gonna survive!*

Gradually my strength returned, and I began a dance, avoiding the creature. It knew I was here and would tear through the forest trying to find me, while I would find places to hide. What added a bit of spice to our game of hide 'n' seek was that the fact that geography of this place shifts from time to time. Nevertheless, I was quickly running out of places to hide when someone new appeared. I heard him stumbling through the undergrowth looking as confused and lost as I must have done when I first arrived. He had short, strawberry blond hair with a matching beard and was wearing a white shirt with a frayed frock coat. He didn't seem to see me as he stopped and looked around.

"I've done it! Ha! I've actually done it!"

He had an English accent, and he began to laugh, but that quickly tapered off as he fully took in his surroundings. There was a faint red halo around him, which is how I knew he had the glimmer, like me.

"Hello there! I'm Mary-Jane Mountmore, but you can call me May!"

He jumped as I approached him.

His name, he told me, was Cyril Snaps, an "occult practitioner" who'd been trying for years to get through to World Ash. His entrance into the realm had come via—of all things—an ornate fireplace in London. He'd spent years learning the incantations and hidden pathways and had finally managed it but "at a terrible cost." He didn't elaborate, and I didn't ask him. But I did ask him what the year was when he traveled over.

"Why, it's 1971!" Cyril said, frowning. "What a queer question."

Which made me realize how much time had passed on the other side. Thinking about how the world might have changed if I could get back there felt like a yoke around my shoulders dragging me down. I had to try to get back before the world I left became unrecognizable to me.

"I have come to explore and to learn!"

Not wanting to dampen his enthusiasm, I explained what I'd learned about the cave and the castle and the general layout of World Ash.

"The castle is the center of this place—this whole screwed-up world revolves around it. That's where we'll find all the answers; that's where the throne of power is!"

I saw a hungry, restless look in his eyes at the mention of power; I saw it with Miles and his coven, and I suspect I'll see it again.

"A cave, you say? And a castle? Extraordinary."

"Why?"

"The fireplace had a number of engravings around it, with a string of symbols that looked like they could be some kind of forgotten language. The engravings—"

"Let me guess. They showed a forest, a cave, a castle, and, probably someplace central, a scary-looking goat?"

He nodded. "How could you—?"

"I'll explain on the way."

"In that case, let's get started!" Cyril clapped his hands together. "Lead the way!"

Which I did.

The location of the cave had already shifted, but it was easy to spot with the red outline at the entrance.

"Fascinating…Fascinating…" Cyril muttered as we walked through the cave.

It didn't look different to any cave I'd seen before, but each to his own.

"I've long been a student of the dark arts and acquired many arcane and rare texts."

"Oh yeah."

Cyril didn't seem to pick up on my indifference.

We reached the rock face. I traced around the symbols again and they began to glow.

"Astounding!"

When I completed the sequence, I pushed against the spongy rock.

"Help me push through!" I called, and Cyril joined me.

At first we were quick, cutting through the mire. We

certainly got further than I had before, and I'm sure I heard Cyril giggling. That didn't last long. The castle was coming into focus when I felt a force like a strong pair of arms pushing me, like before but with more strength. I heard Cyril scream. I forced my head round and saw an energy, a light, racing through him, burning him up. It caught him and twisted him, bubbling his flesh and skinning him. I only saw it for seconds, but I know it will be seared into my mind.

The next thing I knew, I was skidding across the dirt again. That time I did curl up in a ball. I felt sore, and for those freezing, hurting seconds lying in the dirt, I didn't think I'd be able to get up again.

When I was able to bring myself to stop clutching my knees, I found that I wasn't as drained as I had been on my first attempt; it felt like a callus had formed, or scar tissue over a wound. I became more determined to get through to the castle. I set my shoulders square, pulled myself upright, and walked out of the cave.

Godammit! To hell with you! I'm gonna survive!

*

Time was running out. Every time I failed to get to the castle, the goat creature got closer to finding me.

I forget how many of them there were in the end. They'd all have that hungry look in their eyes, they'd get me a little closer to the castle each time, but they'd all burn. Until one day, and one of the more unpleasant visitors. Bullish, with sharp teeth, a musk like spoiled meat, and a bullet head, Bill Salmon barreled through from 1995 with a look of triumph on his face.

When I explained about the cave and the castle, he seemed impatient, like he'd heard it all before, and he walked off as if he knew the way. When he waited for me to catch up, he had the gall to look annoyed with me.

We got to the cave, and he nudged ahead of me but then waited for me at the rock face. I left him waiting for a moment. I don't know if I was expecting an apology; I didn't get one. He just looked at me with a mixture of annoyance and expectation. I couldn't resist a sigh, and then began the all too familiar tracing of the symbols. He was less impressed than the other visitrils, but there was still a trace of something on his face which wasn't arrogance or expectation. As soon as the rock face became malleable, Salmon pushed into it. I didn't mind if this one burned. But, incredibly, we were moving at a pace through the wall, and the castle was more solid, more real. Could this have been…?

And then we were through! We'd got to the other side! The force of my efforts sent me flying and falling to the ground. Like that day my dad pulled me from the sea. Annoyingly, Salmon had managed to stay on his feet.

"Ha!" he said. "I knew—"

But he never got to finish the sentence as he was crushed underneath the weight of a giant cloven hoof. Squashed like a bug.

"Oh." I looked up at the creature I'd been hiding from, its nostrils flaring and its eyes red in the sickly yellow light. I breathed deeply. There was nowhere left to hide. But instead of joining Salmon as an abstract shape in the mud, I saw the creature reach down, and it grabbed me by the scruff of the neck and strode toward the castle with me swinging in its grasp.

If it was gonna kill me, I'd have been dead already, so I was feeling a bit bolder.

"Hey! Hey! I was going there anyway! Hey!" All that time—however long it'd been—all the hiding, did I just need the creature to take me there?

We got to the entrance of the castle, and the huge, misshapen doors—which didn't quite fit the space they were set in—opened of their own accord. As they were opening the creature slung me forward, and it was by luck rather than judgment that I got through the gap. I skidded across the uneven floor and then I found myself looking at two pairs of shoes: one pair was immaculate, shined to a fine polish so that I could see the look of shock on my face; the other pair was scuffed and muddy. I looked up at the owners of the shoes: one was slim, and dressed in a smart, fitted suit; the other was taller and thickset and was dressed in a pair of overalls and a t-shirt and had a scar running across his face. They had similar eyes and mouths, which made me think they were brothers. They were looking straight at me but it was as if they were looking straight through me.

I got to my feet and—'cause I had nothing to lose—opened with my usual gambit.

"I'm Mary-Jane Mountmore, but..."

They just drifted away. That's all I can describe it as. They didn't walk, they *drifted* to the foot of a huge staircase that was annoyingly familiar. The brothers stood in front of it, and at times I could actually see the staircase *through* them. There was a gray pallor about them; I don't just mean their faces, it was their whole bodies that had a washed-out color.

"We know who you are."

Just that simple statement chilled me to the bone. I didn't see either of the figures' lips move, but the deep, gruff voice swirled around me.

"Well, do you mind—"

"We are not truly here, in the same way that you are not truly here. We are only a memory of what we were."

"Well, that makes as much sense as…" But something about what they said—*that you are not truly here*—made my words trail off. I *am* here, aren't I? Standing in front of them I could feel a gnawing anxiety about what happened to me during the moments before I was drawn over here, little flashes of memory. But that could all wait. I was going to survive and get back, whatever it took.

"Why have you brought me here?" I could hear the weariness in my voice.

"We need you to get us back. You're the first person who's been strong enough to get through the rock face."

"What about Bill Salmon?"

The brothers looked at each other. "He wasn't suitable."

Chilling.

"There will be others. We will bring them and test them against the wall. The time will come when the right one will be here, then we shall be free."

The thought of trying that journey again and again made my heart sink.

"What about that creature?"

"That creature is us."

"Right…That makes absolutely no sense."

"When we first traveled over here, this place changed us: it combined us, made us better, stronger. It made us into that creature you see outside."

I'd argue with *better*.

"That's the physical manifestation of us, but World Ash is controlled by the id, by sheer force of will, so we have molded this place."

I looked around. I'd been in better.

"The castle is a constant in this realm. We have constraints on how much we can change it," the voice said as though it was reading my mind. "We will bring others to this realm, you will test them, and one day we will return to the other side."

They disappeared right in front of my eyes, and I heard the misshapen door open behind me. I'd clearly been dismissed, so I tramped out of the castle.

There was a clearing outside, surrounded by nine-foot-high, thick nettles, and in front of me was a rock face, so I didn't know how I was supposed to…

I was pulled toward the rock face and, just as I was about

to slam into it, I once again found myself skidding across the ground outside the cave. But that time I had a sense of purpose.

*

Godammit! To hell with you! I'm gonna survive

*

Marshall

We run along the corridors after Joey. A few times we bump into the back of her as she changes her mind and her direction.

"No! This way!" Conner grabs us by the arms and drags us to the right, into what looks like a solid wall, which we melt through and drop, rolling into a clearing outside the castle.

"How did you know about that?" I ask as I get to my feet.

"Dunno." He shrugs. "I just suddenly thought that was what we had to do."

"Right. Now we need to get as far away from—"

A fucking *tree* is marching toward me.

*

Conner

Out of nowhere, a sick-looking tree strides toward us and grabs Marshall in its branches. He struggles in its clutches until it taps him against its trunk, and he goes limp.

"Oh God!" I hear myself shriek.

"Bind him with the other," says a guttural voice from the castle.

The tree plunges headfirst—do trees even have heads? —

into the rock face and disappears with Marshall. I feel Joey's hand on my shoulder.

"Marshall *will* be okay. I guess from what we heard that he'll be tied up with Davey. If they wanted to kill him, they would have done it already."

"We've got to get after him!" I push at the rock face but now it's as solid as, well, a rock.

"How can't we—"

"I don't know," says Joey. "Maybe the trees can come and go as they please because they're part of the forest? I—"

Another tree grabs hold of both me and Joey and takes us back into the castle.

CHAPTER TWENTY-THREE

Joey

You see, the problem is Davey and Marshall.

It's not their fault, not really. They can't know what it's like for Conner and me, how could they? Although, I've always suspected that Marshall might have a bit of the glimmer about him. For as long as I can remember this "gift" has been like a lead weight tied to my ankle, dragging me down. What gave me some respite from that feeling was meeting Conner. Then Davey came on the scene and things got…complicated. Not in that way. Not really. Conner got it into his head that I betrayed him—and when he gets something into that thick skull of his it's hard to shake—but since all this stuff has happened I've started to wonder: is Conner right, just a little bit? Wow, how annoying would that be!

I never even wanted to do this; it was Davey's idea. He's

always on the hustle, which, when I first met him, I really admired. It wasn't something I could or would do, so I was happy for him to be the face and get us the business. But as time went on, he developed an ugly swagger and wouldn't stop going on about his idea for a TV series. I thought if I was just non-committal that he'd forget about it eventually. But no, he was like a dog with a bone. A TV series? I can't imagine anything worse. It makes me cringe just to think about it, but that's typical of Davey and his pissy machismo. That's why we got lumbered with our stupid name Spirits Unlimited; he did it just to annoy Marshall. Speaking of whom, their idiotic egos have drawn them—and us—into this whole mess.

I may have a way out of this. Oh God, but what if it doesn't work? I could make things worse. But I've got to try.

"We've got to get the Dark Orchid—"

"May."

"May what?"

"Her friends call her May," Conner says, blinking at me.

"I'd hardly say we're friends after what she did, but anyway… We've got to get May on our side."

"Why?"

I've got to be patient with Conner; sometimes he can't see things that are straight in front of him.

"It's why the brothers brought us here to start with. They want to put us in harness and make us work for them, but if we can convince the Dark Orch—sorry, *May*—that they've lied to her, we can work together to defeat the Cruthers."

And there he goes again with the blinking and the chewing of the lip. "Yeah, that could work."

I know he thinks it won't, but I choose to storm ahead. "Right, with Marshall and Davey out of the equation we'll have to work out how to do this ourselves."

"Okay."

We just look at each other.

"So…" I prompt.

We stand in silence again for a few moments.

"Okay, follow me."

We have to negotiate our way around the maze-like structure of the castle. At points it does resemble the Cruthers Hotel, but at others it's sorta like they've given up. It reminds me of when my brother would hold his plastic toy soldiers over a flame to see them melt. They'd end up as a twisted approximation of their former selves. You could still recognize features of what they were within their mangled state; you can sorta see features of the hotel among the organic mess, if you look hard enough.

We're about to walk down one of the jumbled corridors when Conner stops me.

"No, not that way." He looks up and moves his head around as though there's a noise only he can hear. "Can't you hear that?"

I focus, and then, yes, I can hear it; it's the low babble of a voice.

"That's May!" he says. "Follow me!"

We stumble back in the direction we came, swiftly past the room we were held in, and end up in front of a mottled red door. It looks like it's been painted different shades of red over the years and they've started to peel, shedding one layer to reveal another beneath. The door is not a good fit for the frame. It's too small and it's misshapen, letting a sickly yellow light seep through the gap. The door handle looks like the nose of a prizefighter who's been in too many bouts.

We look at each other.

"Ladies first," Conner says, but I get behind him and push.

"Gerroff!" he moans, puts a hand on the door handle, grimaces, wipes his hand on his jeans, and pushes the door open with his sneaker.

We both have to squint to see what's beyond the door: it's what I suppose could be called a set of stairs, but they're lumpy and irregular; it's hard to tell if they're actually man made. The steps descend into darkness.

Conner breathes deeply and closes his eyes. I put a hand on his shoulder, and he smiles, which is something. He takes the first tentative steps in, holding on to the sides for support, and I join him. This is possibly not the most stupid thing we've ever done, but it must be high up on the list. We've taken just four steps when I get the smell of cinnamon, which is a welcome change from some of the other odors I've experienced since I've been in this realm. We get to the bottom and…there's nothing. There's just an empty space, illuminated by a faint purple light. It's not what you'd call a regular room or cellar. The headspace alters in waves: at the bottom of the stairs there's standing room, but at other points you'd have to crawl. Like everything here, it makes no sense, it's more a rabbit warren than a room.

"What are we supposed—" Conner starts. "Hold on, where's that light coming from?"

The light is coming from one of the uneven corners. As it gets brighter, it coalesces into a figure, and then the Dark Orchid—May—comes into sharp focus.

"Oh, hi," she says as though we just popped in for a coffee.

Her greeting wrong-foots me for a moment. "Errr, hello."

She looks a little confused. I don't know if she realizes that she's just materialized There's a purple halo, which fizzles around her.

"You've got to help us!" Conner blurts out. He was never great at negotiations, and before I can say anything he jumps in with "You completely Lando'd us!" which makes her look even more confused.

"What he's saying is that you sold us down the river."

"I've got to survive," the Dark Orchid—when she starts playing ball, maybe I'll remember to call her May—says before adding under her breath, "*Godammit!*"

"I don't get it. How does selling us out to the brothers help you survive?"

The purple halo around her gets darker.

"I've got to get back to the other side. You've seen what it's like out here! It's a living nightmare. I don't even know how long I've been here! Sometimes it feels like days. I met a guy here who said he was from 1971. *1971!* Where you two from, the 21st century?" she says with a snort and we just smile weakly.

Awkward.

"! I dunno what to think, but the brothers have promised they can get me back. But the price…The price is you."

"What can we do?"

"You all managed to get through the barrier, and together we'll have the strength to get them back, and us with them."

"The brothers have lied to you," Conner says, a tremor in his voice.

"You don't understand. *Godammit…*"

"They've used you," I say. Why does Davey pop into my head?

"Like all the rest," she mutters under her breath. Then, with a sigh, she says, "Show me."`

Conner takes my hand and I feel a shudder from him—I can only guess what that's about. "Come on, we have to do this together. It's something you missed when you brought me and Marshall to the castle, something I almost missed…"

I feel him sag, but he rallies and I feel a tingle of energy running through us. We close our eyes and focus, and out of the darkness a new reality swirls into view.

Now we're back in the entrance of the castle and standing in front of us are the Cruthers. Even in their ethereal state they look threatening. Conner is slowing down time so that we can hear what the brothers say. It's so much effort, Conner looks like he's lifting a free weight; sweat is pouring down his face, which is creased with effort. From all around us, just as Conner and Marshall are swept up to join me in my captivity in their dead fish, slowed-down drone we hear them say:

"We finally have everything to break free from this realm and claim our rightful kingdom."

"That doesn't mean anything," May says looking down at her shoes.

"Wake up, May!" Conner says in a surprisingly strident tone. "You mean nothing to them. What do you think they'll do when they get back to the other side? They'll discard you, me, her, like trash."

"No, I've helped them out, they'll…"

"Come on, stop kidding yourself."

Her shoulders slump and she lets out a sigh, which sends out a sparking wave of purple light across the room.

"I'm gonna call you May now…" There's nothing else for it; I can't keep this from her. "I don't know how to tell you this, May, but you can't go back."

The glare from the purple light almost blinds us.

"I don't believe you!"

I feel a wave of energy pound into me, which nearly knocks us off our feet, but Conner and I cling to each other and manage to stay upright.

"I can show you," I say. "You can never go back."

"No!" screams May.

Another wave hits us, but we manage to stay on our feet. Just. A curtain of flecks and sparks brushes across the room in the wake of the wave.

Now it's my turn to present

what I saw just before I was brought over: what the energy from the window did to May, how it eviscerated her. It's like Conner and I are actually in the corridor, but May is there with us, watching events unfurl, reliving something that she can't, or won't remember. Then as though her strings have been cut, she collapses to the floor. May curls up in a ball and starts to sob. We hear her muttering "No, no, no." to herself through the tears as she rocks back and forth, finally after a few minutes she uncurls, and gets back on her feet. May straightens her shoulders and brings her hands together before flinging them apart.

"I don't believe it!" she screams, sending another wave, which brings us back to the cellar and knocks us to the ground.

Conner gets unsteadily to his feet, and puts an arm out to help me up, and in the process, I nearly pull him back down. When he's upright he's weaving as if he's had too much to drink. He reaches out an arm to find something to steady himself, but there isn't anything, so I put my arm around him for support, which makes him smile and seems to give him confidence.

"You knew, though, didn't you? Deep down. That day when we first met."

"It can't be true."

"You know it is."

"It's another illusion in this funhouse." says May.

"It's not, we're not lying to you." Conner replies.

"I don't know what to do anymore."

"Help us, help us fight the brothers."

"Yes, yes." Another sigh. "I will help you fight the Cruthers. God help me."

She seems to glide across the ground toward us and take us by the shoulders. She has a surprisingly firm grip.

"Let's go."

*

Conner

We're winding our way through the melty, funhouse corridors of the castle with May leading the way. She's moving so rapidly that we have to run to keep up; she's doing that odd gliding thing, so it's hardly fair.

"Why are we moving so fast?"

"We've gotta get out of here as soon as we can. This is the Cruthers' domain, made by their sheer will."

You'd think that if they could make anything, perhaps they'd make something a little nicer than this.

"We've got to get back out into the forest if we stand any chance of beating them."

"But why—"

A tremble goes through the corridor, followed by a roar, stopping Joey's question.

May looks frightened. "They know. They're coming for us."

May gets behind us and gives us a push. It's not a push; it's an almighty force. I glance behind us and she has her palms facing us and there's a purple light shooting out from them. It's like being on a roller coaster, but a really screwed-up, terrifying roller coaster. I know all roller coasters are supposed to be terrifying, but you know those fairgrounds you see occasionally that have seen better days? The signs are missing letters, and the coaster has flaking paint, is rusted, and may have a few slats missing? Yeah, this is one of those roller coasters. It looks as though we're going to slam into one of the castle's sludgy walls when, at the last second, we swerve to the right. I think I can hear Joey screaming before I realize that it's actually me screaming. I don't know how May can tell all the corridors apart as we rush past them; they all look the same to me. I close my eyes at one point but that's even more horrifying.

"We're nearly there!" May shouts as we speed toward an imposing set of misshapen double doors. But before we can hurtle through them, the brothers step out and block the way.

"Where do you think you're going?" says Milán with a whisper of a smile, as we come to a juddering halt.

Joey and I fall forward in an undignified heap while May faces the brothers.

A fiery purple light shoots over our heads toward the brothers, but it goes straight through them. Milán smiles and Jan laughs as they both unleash their own bolt of crimson fire toward May. Joey and I stay down as the bolt flies over us, but I can feel it burn the hair on the back of my neck. I look back and see the fire hit May square in the stomach. She lets out a yelp of pain, grows dim, and falls back, but manages to stay on her feet, like a fighter on the ropes. And like a fighter, she springs back.

"You need me! Remember? You need me!"

Now Milán joins in with the laughter as May starts to run toward them. On the way, she grabs Joey and me by the scruff of our necks. For a nanosecond the brothers look shocked, then ready themselves to unleash another blast at May. They don't seem to care that they might hit us. Is May just going to try and run through them? 'Cause they suddenly look a lot more solid. Just as I think we're about to find out, she swerves to the right and we melt into the wall. We seem to pass through a cloud, then we're rolling and tumbling back into the clearing before the rock face portal to the cave.

"How do we—" starts Joey, but it seems to be her day for getting cut off, because no sooner have we started to get to our feet than May is hurling us at the seemingly solid rock.

"FUUUUUUU—" shouts Joey, but we bounce into the rock rather than bounce off it.

The rock has become like Jell-O, and I can see May's reflection in it. Now that we've escaped the castle she has lost that eerie ability to glide and, in her haste to join us, she nearly trips and falls. She regains her balance and leaps into the Jell-O rock just as the brothers enter the clearing. They look angry and fire off an energy shot, just before I feel the jolt of May joining us. As we try and push through back into the cave, the energy bolt hits the rock face and has the effect of a cue ball hitting other balls: it sends the three of us spinning off. I can see May and Joey tumbling off in opposite directions, growing more distant by the second. In this bizzarro space that isn't a space I have a stab of terror. We could be spinning away from each other for eternity. Lost in this amorphous womb.

No.

I picture the three of us and move through the space as if it was water. I make a physical effort, like I'm swimming, and I can see the other two doing the same thing. Gradually we move toward each other, despite the continued depth charges of the Cruthers' energy bolts. We're within touching distance when a wave ripples through the space. I can see from the terror in May's eyes that the brothers must have joined us. She grabs mine and Joey's hand and pulls. It feels like she pulls us upwards, but it's hard to tell. We're moving, though, and with a joint effort we fall back into the cold, earthy cave like we've just surfaced from the sea, spluttering and taking deep breaths. We don't have time to find our bearings as May grabs us again by the scruff of our necks and drags us forward. The first few steps are half running, half standing up.

"The brothers won't be able to follow us through to the cave," May says.

"You sure?" asks Joey. "Cause they seemed to be pretty intent on following us."

"No, it's just bluster. What we saw was just a projection of the brothers; that version of them can't move much further than the castle."

"*Are* you sure of that?" I'm certainly not.

"Pretty sure."

"Why are we running?"

"You can't be too careful."

We burst out of the cave into the fetid air of the forest, but still it's good to be back here, away from the castle and away from the brothers. However, the forest is still as wrong as it was before, and still bathed in that sickly yellow light. I put my hands on my knees and try to get my breath back. Joey and May seem to have recovered already.

I walk ahead. I don't want to talk to Joey. Being out of immediate danger has brought everything tumbling back. The lies. The betrayal.

"Where we going?" she asks.

"Dunno. Somewhere." I keep walking.

"I suppose you rescued me."

"Typical," I mutter under my breath.

"What?"

"Nothing. Let's keep walking."

"We have to talk to each other if we want to get through this."

"Don't have to," I mumble.

"What?"

"Nothing." I walk a few more steps before I notice that Joey's not walking beside me. I turn around and she's stopped still with her arms folded. "What now?" I say with a sigh.

"Come on, you've got something on your mind."

"Do you really want to know?"

"Yes."

"Do you *really*?"

"Yes, really."

"Why should I trust you?" I chew my lip and there's the taste of copper in my mouth.

"Now's not the time."

"Now's exactly time." She sighs.

This has been brewing for a while, but I'm not sure how to begin.

"Right, look, I don't know what grudge you've been holding for all these years but you never gave me a chance to explain. You just shut me out."

"Can you blame me after what you did?"

"What did I do?"

"You stabbed us in the back and took all the glory. You only thought about yourself."

"That's bullshit, and you never let me explain. I reached out to you and you just shut me off. We could have all been in it together: you, me, Marshall, and Davey. Just think what a team we would have made!"

"You're just saying that."

"No, I'm not. It's not too late for us."

It's not too late for us? For *us*? Oh God, don't give me hope. I my acid reflux begins to act up.

"Okay, okay." I blush and it feels like a wave is crashing against me. "That may be true. I'll work with you for now. Doesn't mean I have to trust you."

"Why, aren't *you* the magnanimous overlord!"

This does make me laugh.

"What do we do now?" she asks, and instinctively I turn to

ask Marshall, but he's not there and I don't have my antacids.

Joey reaches out, takes my hand, and smiles. Suddenly it feels like everything is going to be fine.

"Don't worry, we'll work it out together."

"Right, right," I say, still catching my breath and turning to include May. "What's the plan? How do we fight the Cruthers?"

"What I suggest—" May starts, but a blast of something swiping past us cuts her short, and then she's gone, she's disappeared.

Joey and I look at each other, then look up. Standing over us is the goat creature, breathing heavily through its moist nostrils as it glares down on us. It's bringing down its left arm, which looks like a knotted piece of rope with tufts of hair sticking out.

"Oh God, it's just swept May aside." I hear Joey say.

What's it going to do to us?

CHAPTER TWENTY-FOUR

World Ash, "1914"

Milán and Jan crashed through the portal into the forest of World Ash, landing with a heavy thud, causing Jan to groan.

"Brother?" he said in a weak rasp.

Milán's hands and clothes were drenched in his brother's blood. Jan's face was white, there were black lines underneath eyes unable to focus on his brother, and a rattling noise came out of his mouth every time he took a breath.

Milán cradled his dying brother in his arms. This was not how it was supposed to end. He looked around for help that wasn't there. Instead, he was surrounded by ash-gray trees.

This is what we spent all this time, money, and blood to get to? This is *it*?

Jan was trying to say something. Milán had to press his

ear against his brother's lips to hear.

"We did it, brother! We did it! We got here!" he whispered.

"Yes, yes we did."

Milán wondered if Jan knew he was dying—he had never been the sharpest of tools—then felt instantly ashamed. The truth was he had been looking after his brother their entire lives, ever since their mother had died in the old country, and at times it had felt like a burden to be shouldered. Although Jan had the physical presence, in many ways he was very naïve, and Milán had felt a burning resentment at having to look out for him. But now, with his brother's life ebbing away in his arms, he felt an icy terror at the prospect of being left alone.

Jan's blood flowed down his arms and soaked into the ground of the forest. Milán looked on in disbelief as the foliage began to creep toward them. The trees were getting closer. They sent out roots and vines, snaking across the ground, hungry for life and blood.

"No!" Milán snarled. And he fought them.

The vines wrapped themselves around his limbs and pierced his skin and soaked up his brother's blood. A shiver of delight rippled through the forest. Milán pulled the small book with a brown leather cover which he'd gained from Nestor from his torn jacket and started to read the incantation.

"No, brother, no! It should be two people reading…" Jan rasped, too late.

The image of the Baphomet goat shines out from the rock face with a golden hue . The light burned away the roots and vines trying to merge with the brothers, but Milán began to scream as it started to stretch his skin and bones, the book falling from his hand. It was like his skin was a piece of canvas being pulled over a frame. Jan was too weak to scream and could only utter a low groan as he could feel his bones grow within his body. At the same time both brothers could feel their flesh and bones becoming malleable. The color of the beam changed from gold to a deep crimson. As the brothers began to grow, their bodies began to meld and change. Their two screaming faces melted together and the image of the goat's features superimposed itself onto the waxy, bubbling, amalgamated head of the brothers. The lumpy combination of the three began to solidify into a goat's head, but with features from the brothers. In the middle of its forehead, as though branded on the flesh, was an angry, red scar in the form of a pentangle. The shoulders of the new creature broadened out, the legs thickened, and the feet morphed into hooves. The last vestiges of the brothers' humanity were shredded along with their clothes, which were torn to rags. The creature flexed its new muscles beneath its matted, thick fur. At over twenty foot, it towered over the forest.

The new three-eyed chimera had been birthed into World Ash. It looked out at its domain, a jumble of thoughts in its newly joined mind. The one thing the newborn knew for sure was that it wanted to get back to the old world.

It roared, saliva raining in ribbons from its mouth onto the ground. The roar echoed around, and the forest trembled.

CHAPTER TWENTY-FIVE

Conner

So this is how it ends, squashed under the hoof of a freaky giant goat thing in an occult dimension. It's not the strangest death I could have had to be honest, but it's pretty close. I feel Joey's hand reach out and take mine as we wait for the inevitable.

But the inevitable doesn't come.

"You!" The creature points one of its misshapen "fingers" at us. Its rasping growl sounds as though it's not used to speaking.

"Home! You!" It leans its goaty face close to us, and we both recoil at its foul, fetid breath. It reminds me of the last conversation I had with Marv about Roswell.

"I think…I think it wants us to get it through the portal."

The creature leans back and roars its approval, which echoes around the forest.

"Okay then, but on one condition." I try to keep the tremble out of my voice. And fail.

The creature roars, throws out a hand and cuts a tree in two. I don't think it's happy, but I press on.

"You must return Marshall to me."

"And Davey," Joey adds.

"S'pose so." I mumble, but Captain Goaty has already picked both of us up and is stomping through the forest, bulldozing its way through trees and thickets.

We're dangling inches from the dirt. I try my best to avoid the sharp thorns, which tear at my clothes as we speed by. When I'm not trying to stop myself being ripped to shreds, I attempt to orient myself, but I don't recognize any of our surroundings. We come to a sudden stop and the creature hurls us into the undergrowth. More by luck than design, I suspect, our landing is cushioned by some plants. When we stand up, we can see the tree holding Davey; now it's holding Marshall too, and both are unconscious; breathing, but very pale. The creature roars in the direction of the tree and nothing happens. It roars again and stamps one of its hooves, and slowly the tree withdraws its branches from Marshall and Davey, who slump to the ground. They shift as if they'd passed out from a heavy night and were trying to get moving. The creature grunts, turns around, and walks slowly back through the tunnel it's made in the forest. It turns its monstrous head toward us and roars.

"I think it wants us to follow." Joey says. We scoop up our hazy comrades and stumble after it.

It feels like we're Napoleon's troops retreating across Russia as we shuffle along in the creature's wake, stopping occasionally when either Davey or Marshall stumble.

"We've got to find out what that smell in the apartment is… It could be a dead rat…I dunno…maybe?" Marshall mumbles at me.

"Don't worry, we'll figure it out." I tell him.

He smiles, nods, and stumbles on.

Eventually we arrive back where we came in, only without Eugene's puzzled face looking through the rock face. Joey and I let Davey and Marshall drop to the ground.

The creature roars at us. We know what's expected of us.

"Ready?" she asks me.

I nod.

When I touch Joey's hand it's like touching a live wire. A jolt goes through me like I've been plunged into an ice-cold bath. I can see a shimmering halo twisting around my fingers and dancing around Joey. I glance to my left and see the rock face glow and begin to pulsate. The creature begins to mew with pleasure. It reaches out and touches the rock face, which has become pliable like rubber. I look at Joey and nod. A breeze rustles through the leaves, and through the trees shines a purple light, which the creature at first doesn't seem to notice.

"Hush…"

A voice rolls across the ground. And at the heart of the purple light, with her arms outstretched, is May, the Dark Orchid.

"You're not leaving this place."

Purple tendrils stretch out from her fingers and weave their way around the creature, sending it into a frenzy of activity, dropping Marshall and Davey in its efforts to rip free of the Dark Orchid's web.

We scoop up the fallen hostages and hobble toward the rock face. The glow has begun to fade, and it's still struggling. May is entwining it with flames of purple light and trying to pull it back, which further enrages the creature. They almost seem to be in a dance, bobbing around each other. Have they done this dance before? Joey and I make a half run, half limp movement as we move Marshall and Davey across the uneven ground toward the portal. I can feel the ground beneath me tremble under the force of the battle going on behind us.

"I can't!" Joey yells. "He's a dead weight!"

My hands are full, but I head back to help. A tree falls just inches away from us, a casualty of the creature's struggle. Joey and I link arms and use our combined strength to drag our—respective—friends to the rock face. I hear a strangled cry from Joey as the portal gets ever smaller.

"We're not going to reach it in time!" she yells.

CHAPTER TWENTY-SIX

Conner

It looks hopeless.

With still too much ground to cover before the portal closes, a strong breeze catches us, carrying us forward, with a purple light glimmering in the fetid air. We move with such speed that we don't get time to take a breath. We're speeding toward the rock face.

"No! No! No!"

"Shit! Shit! Shit!"

It's hard to know who's saying what.

I close my eyes and clench my teeth, waiting for an impact which never comes.

We find ourselves tumbling onto the carpet of floor six and a half of the Cruthers Hotel. All four of us are tangled up in an undignified heap like we've been involved in a frenetic game of Twister that has gone very wrong. Marshall and Davey are still passed out. Joey and I untangle ourselves, apologizing constantly and trying not to make eye contact, then we start laughing and hug for a maybe bit too long, unhand each other, and stand up to look at the window, which still has an unearthly glow.

"Oh God, I thought when we were heading toward the rock face that we were…"

"Me too!"

"It was like being on a roller coaster!"

I become aware of presence. I turn around slowly.

"Thank GodI It's only Eugene! We…"

Something has changed about Eugene. He seems to have grown, although he's probably just standing upright. But it looks like someone has turned up the definition on him; he seems *sharper*. He's got a steely look in his eyes and a gun in his hand.

"Oh no," I say.

"'Fraid so," he says with a shrug. "I was hoping that this wasn't going to be necessary, but there you go. I thought that Dwayne and the others would be able to take care of this, but - " he shrugs " - if a job's worth doing..."

"Why are you doing this?"

"Come on, Conner, I thought you were supposed to be the smart one who can read minds."

"It comes and goes."

"He's the head of the Infidels' coven," Joey says.

"See! She gets it!"

He was hiding in plain sight.

"Now you're going to bring the Cruthers back, or I'll start shooting into bits of your friends."

"You don't understand what's on the other side of the window. They aren't even human anymore. They—"

He fires the gun, which sends a cloud of dust up by Marshall's thigh.

"I know full well what's beyond that window and what the Cruthers have become: *better* than human. Finally, the Infidels will get the respect we deserve. We'll show people what we can do. And *now* you'll bring the Cruthers back to claim their kingdom." Eugene aims the gun at Marshall's crotch. "I won't ask again."

I pull the small leather bound book I found in World Ash out of my pocket and open it. Joey and I begin to recite the incantation, the window begins to bulge, and out of the glass comes the familiar hooves of the goat–Cruthers creature as it begins to pull itself through to our world.

The look on Eugene's face is one of ecstasy. His mouth is cracked into a Joker smile and his arms are flung wide to welcome the creature. He looks like he's going to cry in joy.

"I've waited so long for this day! I never thought it would happen!"

It's like he's accepting an Oscar. I look around and the entire corridor seems to have become spongy and I can feel myself begin to hyperventilate.

There's a sharp BANG!

A plume of blood spurts from Eugene's shoulder as he's pushed back. Behind us, with a smoking gun, is Murray. She's got a few cuts and some dust on her, but otherwise looks unharmed. She runs past us keeping her gun trained on the crumpled form of Eugene. He looks like he's trying not to cry by screwing up his face, but it's having the opposite effect. He has a hand over the wound on his shoulder to stem the flow of blood.

"Oh, you're going to pay for that!" he snivels, with snot running down his face. He doesn't really epitomize menace.

"I've got the gun and the badge, and you…Just saying."

"You—"

"No." Murray cuts him off. "I'm the one asking the questions. Why did you murder Goldstein, Angela Maron and Professor Nash?"

The sniveling stops. Eugene looks genuinely surprised. "What?"

"You heard , why—"

"I *heard* what you said!" he shouts. "I don't understand. We didn't murder anyone. Why would we?"

"You tell me."

"I *am* telling you, you stupid bitch!" he snarls. "We didn't—"

A sound like chicken leg being torn from a carcass drowns out Eugene and brings our attention back to the window.

The goat creature is almost free and in our world.

May's efforts haven't been enough. We've lost. We only have darkness ahead of us.

CHAPTER TWENTY-SEVEN

Murray is in combat pose—legs apart, shoulders back—and she's pointing her gun at the creature. She lets off three shots, which find their target, and blood is coursing from the torso of the creature. It writhes around in the window trying to get purchase to pull itself through.

It can't be this easy to stop, can it?

Well, no it can't. Before our eyes, the blood trickles back in and the wounds heal. The creature retrieves the bullets from its fur and flicks them back. They whizz by, narrowly missing us. For the first time I see some human emotion in the creature's eyes, and it is absolutely incandescent rage. It lands in the corridor, flailing around in a storm of fury.

"Run!"

Murray doesn't have to say that twice and we run blind—well, we actually follow Joey, who just rushes into the first room she can find. We leave Marshall and Davey where they are, there's nothing we can do for them at the moment. The creature pursues us – and thankfully ignores our colleagues - and throws its whole bulk against the door, but it's too big to get through. Cracks appear in the masonry and splinters of wood from the door ping through the air and fall to the floor.

The creature lets loose a scream of anger and frustration, which shakes some more masonry. As it continues to throw its bulk against the door, I hear wood tearing and know it won't be long until it gets in. We all look around for a way out, but we're cornered.

"Come with me," says Murray as she and heads toward a window – which must have been added as part of the refurb - pulls it open and climbs through.

Joey follows her without a hesitation. I'm not so sure, until another thump, as the creature throws itself at the door again, makes me scamper to join them. It's biting cold as I edge out. Oh God, can I do this? I take a deep breath and step through, and instantly wish I hadn't. I thought there'd be an external fire escape or something, but all I can see is Murray and Joey with their backs to the outside of the building, slowly moving along a tiny strip of ledge.

It must be a good seventy-foot drop down there.

God, I can't think about that.

I look back into the room. I can hear the creature getting

ready to throw itself at the door again, and this time it'll get in.

I close my eyes and start moving.

My right foot slips and I open my eyes and start to hyperventilate and feel giddy. There's a loud crash from behind me and I know that the creature has broken through.

Oh God, oh God!

But the most overwhelming calm flows over me, like a duvet covering me on a cold and rainy morning.

I can do this.

I look over at Joey and I know that she's responsible for my sudden Zen-like state. We exchange a shaky smile and I calmly edge my way around the building.

Murray is the first of us to negotiate the tricky corner of the hotel.

I *can* do this.

Despite Joey's help, I can feel my acid indigestion flaring up like Mount Vesuvius.

Murray has slipped around the corner and now it's Joey's turn, careful and slow.

I'm on the approach when I hear a deafening roar. I don't want to look but I can't help myself. The creature is trying to force itself through the window "Here's Johnny!" style, and it'll manage it, soon. Its head is out and it's trying to pull its arms through.

I can feel the cool brick of the hotel against my palms and decide to concentrate on that and not think about the rumbles coming from my right.

With deep breaths and calm peppered with stabs of acid and anxiety, I start to ease my way to the corner, just as a pigeon comes to say hello. I try to nudge it off but it begins to aggressively peck my sneaker. I try to kick it, only to have a heart-stopping slip before getting my grip back. Thankfully the pigeon gets bored and flies off. Inching my way around, the New York wind flutters through my clothes. Safely on the straight again, I see Joey and Murray climbing the external fire escape I'd hoped would be outside the window. Why did they put it so far away? I'm just grateful to see it. I reach out and put one foot on the rung. I feel a sharp tug on my other leg. I look behind me. The creature has grasped hold of my leg and is pulling me toward it. I kick out but it holds fast. It's shredding my jeans. I try to kick again but that does nothing.

"Help!"

Joey grabs my arm and tries to pull me back toward the ladder, but it does nothing to help.

I feel something whistle past me and a red hole explodes in the middle of the creature's head. All three eyes cross to look at the hole.

Murray is holding onto the metal staircase with one hand and aiming her gun, smoke curling out of the barrel, with the other.

For a horrible moment I think it's going to swat off a direct shot to the head like it's a flea bite, but its grip melts away, the creature goes limp, and it tumbles off the ledge, bouncing off the building with a sickening thump of flesh hitting masonry.

The three of us scrabbling down the fire escape causes it to make an alarming creaking noise. Murray heaves herself down the last few rungs and looks like she disappears back into the hotel through a window. She's quickly followed by Joey.

God, I'll be glad to get back into the hotel, away from creatures from another realm, the cold, and homicidal New York pigeons. The window back into the hotel is in sight when I hear a roar that sounds like thunder.

"Oh God."

I look behind me and groan. Clawing its way up the building, digging its talons into the flesh of the hotel, and making its way up toward me is the creature. The bullet wound in its head is nothing more than a graze now. I rush to get to the window just as it nearly catches up.

I make a real dog's breakfast of getting in. I put it squarely down to panic. For some reason I think it's best to put one leg in at a time, whereas I should have just dived in. After I put my right leg in, I get flustered and put my left-hand in.

"Let us help you," Murray says, reaching out.

"I'm fine."

I try to hurry, but slip and tumble in and fall over myself, landing squarely on my face. Joey looks away, but I can still see her laughing. It annoys me, but I can't blame her.

"I'm fine I'm fine," I say, springing up, which only goes to emphasize my embarrassment.

I slam the window down behind me.

"We've got to get moving, it's climbing up the building!"

I can feel the room begin to shake. We run out into the corridor.

"Where are we going now?" Joey asks.

"We've got to get to the roof."

CHAPTER TWENTY-EIGHT

I look around. We're cornered. We only have one option. I elbow open the door to the service stairs and we dash through it.

"Why do we need to get to floor six and a half?" asks Murray.

"I'm sure there's another nexus point there says Joey. Before Davey and I were pulled into World Ash, we were attacked by all sorts of visions. Davey saw them, too, and he doesn't have the glimmer, so it must have been something else. Not quite a portal, maybe, but the fabric between our world and World Ash seems to be thin up there; we might be able to force the creature back."

"Follow me!" I say and run up the stairs.

I'm nearly knocked off my feet when more ghosts from days gone by hit me: the Infidels fighting with the Mescaleros, a last desperate fight, the culmination of a war that saw the streets of the city splattered with the blood of the innocent and guilty in equal measure. It's so vivid that it feels like I've been pushed back through time. I recognize the younger Cruthers brother, but he's not the figure from the painting: he's caked in sweat and blood; I can almost smell it. He's trying to get away from his assailant with the Baphomet centerpiece under his arm. Trying to get to his brother and sensing the end.

I close my eyes and focus. I need to be in the present.

This must be a barrier that the creature is throwing at us to try and stop us. But stop us from what?

With a smack I'm back in the present and the creature can only be seconds away from us. I grab Joey's hand and pull her up the stairs. I don't know why, but I know we have to get to the rooftop.

"Get off me!" Joey screams.

I don't know if she's caught up in the same visions, but I need to get her out of whatever trap the creature has got her in. I take her head in my hands, look into her eyes, and, with all my might, think, *I trust you. Please come with me.*

She snaps back, smiles, and we bound up the stairs, with Murray following. I can hear the creature behind us. The door that leads to the roof looks very closed. We look at each other, laugh, and both throw ourselves at the door, crashing through to the roof. We slide through pigeon guano and look around.

"Wow, the maintenance guys haven't been up here in a while," says Joey.

There's an amazing vista across the New York skyline and the city going about its business—never anything other than frenetic, the ever-present buzz of activity, blissfully unaware of what's about to happen to it—and I'm looking out at it with Joey. God, I wish I had the time to really share this with her.

There's a crash of shredding wood and masonry as the creature tears through the door. We rush away and hide behind a dented water tower that has seen better days. I look around, behind us is the creature and in front of us is a God-knows how many stories drop.

We have nowhere left to run.

"I think I know what we need to do."

"Yeah. Me, too. And surely, if we've already released the creature into the world, there can't be any *more* horrors to unleash. Can there?"

This is answered by a deafening KLANG! as the creature throws itself against the other side of the water tower. I take the battered brown leather book from underneath my hoodie and turn to the page of the incantations.

"See you on the other side."

She smiles at me and we begin to chant together, trying the best with what's written down.

"Gate gate paragate parasamgate bodhi svaha!

Oṃ namo bhagavatyai ārya prajñāpāramitāyai!!

The effect is instant: a rush of power as we say the words and they spring out from the yellowing pages. Colors fly around and the air crackles and fizzes with energy like space dust.

There's a howl of anger and pain from the creature as the energy generated from our words wraps it in sparking tendrils. It struggles to release itself but the more it struggles the more wrapped up it gets, like the trees in World Ash.

A vortex forms behind the creature, which is dragged toward it. I can glimpse World Ash at the heart of the swirl. The creature rages against the tendrils and holds onto the water tower, but the energy is so great that it becomes untethered and flies toward the energy hole. It manages to dig its hooves into the roof. It gains temporary purchase but can't hold out against the pull of the tendrils, and makes deep furrows as it's dragged along.

"Great!" I shout, but the vortex is getting bigger and its pull is getting stronger. Anything that isn't bolted down is being pulled into it, and then things which *are* bolted down head into it.

"How do we close it?" I scream.

Joey frantically looks through the book for an answer, but there isn't one. And then the book gets plucked out of her hand and sucked into the vortex. She doesn't have time to react as she's picked up and begins to get in behind it. I grab hold of her and wrap my other hand around a nearby strut, but I can feel myself being lifted off my feet. The vortex is growing bigger and dragging more in with it. Joey's shouting something in the maelstrom but I can't hear her. I can't hold on. I can hear cracking and I don't know if it's what I'm clinging onto or my bones.

Just as my fingers are prized from what I'm holding onto, some familiar purple tendrils snake and swirl out of the vortex and begin to pull against its nebulous edges to close it, sending ripples like heat waves on a hot horizon across the rooftop. But it's too late. I lose my grip, and Joey and I tumble toward the swirling gateway to World Ash.

CHAPTER TWENTY-NINE

Conner

I t's like rushing down a water slide but not as much fun. I can actually see the gnarled, wrong-looking trees of World Ash, inches from my nose.

There's a shift from a water slide to a roller coaster as I'm thrown around. Joey flies past me with one of the purple tendrils wrapped around her midriff. I look around and see the overcast, polluted Manhattan sky. May is trying to keep us safe as well as closing the vortex, but we're being hurled around the roof.

I think I'm going to be sick. I can hear the crackle of energy around the vortex as we get closer and it gets smaller. Bits of debris swirl around us, and a razor-thin sheet of metal misses Joey by inches, before disappearing into World Ash.

We're inches from the vortex and it's still large enough to

swallow the both of us. A wave of energy flows through the tendrils holding us, and an almost blinding flash of purple light throws us across the roof. We land with an "Oomf!" as the wind is knocked out of me. It's not *the* most undignified thing that's happened to me in the last thirty-six hours.

The vortex finally disappears with a POP!

In that moment after, the pigeons sound like hawks.

"Did that just happen?" Joey asks.

"I guess so?" We both look at the spot where only seconds ago was a portal to another world.

Joey is grimacing and rubbing her shoulder.

"You okay?"

She smiles and nods. "You?"

Good point. I tentatively stand up. Apart from aches and pains I'm fine, although my acid reflux is acting up again.

"Nothing broken." Which I follow up with a laugh.

Joey joins in, and I walk over and help her up. The atmosphere on top of the roof feels like a storm has passed, and there's a lingering chemical smell, which must have come from the vortex.

The silence feels like drinking an ice-cold glass of water on a hot summer day. Actually, it's not quiet. I can hear birds chirping. I haven't heard a bird chirping since I got dragged into World Ash. I don't think I've ever paid attention to birds singing before. It's gorgeous. Why have I never noticed this before?

*

Marshall and Davey are where we left them. Murray hunches down to check on them, as Marshall is slowly coming round. He's opening his eyes wide and trying to pull himself upright, looking around with a bewildered expression on his face. While I wait for him to come back to the land of the living, there's something on my mind. Joey is checking on Davey, who's still out cold but apart from that seems fine.

"What now?" I ask her.

"As soon as I can get Davey into a cab I'm going home. I'm going to run a hot bath and pour a cold glass of wine and try to put this behind me."

"That's not what I mean. I mean what about us?"

"There is no *us*, there never was an *us*."

"I didn't mean it like that."

"What *did* you mean it like?"

Good question. I start to chew my lip. "What I mean is… what I mean *is*…that when we were back there"—I tilt my head toward the broken window—"I thought we got something back, something we had before, something lost when Davey came along, before all that—you know—stuff." I'm stumbling over my words like I've got a mouth full of marbles, but then Joey smiles.

"Are you trying to say that you might be beginning to trust me? Well, I am honored."

"I wouldn't go that far," I say.

We laugh and it feels good.

"Yeah, something happened over there. Let's see what

happens. But it's a start." She squeezes my hand and I could sing with joy. "You've got to talk to me, Conner. You can't just hold onto stuff; you'll give yourself an ulcer."

Too late.

"What you've got, what *we've* got is a gift, a talent; you've got to stop seeing it as something to put up with."

"S'pose so."

"No *suppose* about it. Look at what we've just done! We can be a real force for good, really help people."

"Yeah, well…" I say, looking down at my trainers. "You're the one chasing the dollars." When I look back up, she's rubbing the back of her neck.

"Yeah, I've started thinking about that. Being over there it's—I dunno—it's given me a different perspective on things. Maybe it's time to make changes. Just think what a team you and I could make!"

"What about Marshall and Davey?"

"Let's be honest, what do they bring to the table?"

"Marshall's helped me a lot, and…"

"Yes?"

"Uhhh…and he's got mad IT skills?" It feels like a weak defense. We've been through a lot together, but is Joey right?

"I didn't want to do this."

"What do you mean?" I ask.

"I didn't want to take this case. As soon as we walked into the Cruthers I was begging him to leave." She jabs a finger in Davey's direction. He's rubbing his head and looking around.

"But no, he insisted that we do this. He's got this whole *vision* for us, but I've started to think it's *his* vision. He wouldn't listen to me, and because of that this whole thing happened."

I don't think she's being quite fair, but maybe she's got a point. Could I live without Marshall?

"Anyway, think about it. Imagine it: you and me together." She sighs. "I've gotta…" and she nods her head toward Davey, who attempts to stand on his own two feet and fails.

Joey walks off. She turns her head and over her shoulder and says, "See you round the clubs."

*

Marshall

I still feel groggy but considering what I've been through I feel better than could be expected.

We must do something to honor the Dark Orchid. We must do something to honor *May*. And I know exactly what it is.

*

Considering Atherton isn't too keen on the legacy of the Cruthers, he didn't seem so happy about my suggestion, but I made it part of my agreement and he reluctantly agreed.

We're in the reception area and bump into Marv. Well, I say we bump into Marv; he's basically hanging about and pulls his "Oh, fancy meeting you here!" move.

"Oh, hi!"

"Hey, Marv."

"What are you doin' there?" he asks.

"It's pretty obvious, isn't it."

If I'm being a bit of a prick with Marv, it's because I've unscrewed the portrait of the Cruthers, but it's still refusing to come away. Conner brought the BPoD and so, with a bit of grunting and effort with various tools, we manage to pull it off the wall along with a big chunk of the hotel itself. The Cruthers are not going gently into that good night.

"What are you going to do with it?" Marv asks.

"We're going to take it to a good home." I need to get off this topic pretty quickly. "What news about the refurbishment?"

Marv brightens up. "Oh, it's good news. All the business that's been happening on floor six and a half has gone viral. Bookings are way up, so I've heard. So the word on the street—"

Word on the street? Yeah, you're a real playa Marv.

"—is that what they're planning now is to actually use the hotel's legacy as a hook to bring visitors in - ghost tours and the like. It's a bit corny but…" Marv shrugs.

"What does Atherton think about that?"

"Oh, he's not happy about it." Marv chuckles. "But it came from the backers so he had to fall into line. He'll find a way to spin it so it was his idea. You seen Eugene?"

Conner and I shrug.

Now that we've removed the Cruthers from their gloomy enclave we can replace them with another painting. A painting of May. As soon as we hang the painting it feels like the entire reception area lets out a big sigh of relief. I stare at the painting for a moment and think about May and where is now. Is she still dancing with the creature? Conner and I look at each other and nod. Now to sort out the Cruthers—or, rather, their portrait.

We take it five blocks away from the hotel to a rubbish-strewn alleyway. We walk into the gloom, making sure that no can see us from the main drag. I prop their portrait up against the wall and splash lighter fluid over it.

"Take that, you fucks!" I say as I strike a match and throw it at the painting.

But the fire doesn't seem to want to take the brothers. In fact, it doesn't catch at all, and it takes a further six lit matches and me actually going right up to the painting before it goes up in flames. It's as though their scowls are putting out the fire. But boy, when it goes up it goes up! It singes my eyebrows 'cause I can't step away quick enough.

The brothers' faces contort in the flames, and for one brief moment it looks as though they merge and change into the image of that hideous goat. I run a hand over my face and, as the portrait turns to ash, I look at Conner.

"I need a drink."

*

Atherton

I wait till they've all gone.

The Minty Library. I walk in there and up to the fireplace and run my fingers around the cold metal details. I look behind me and check again that there's no one around. From my pocket I take a small, knotted piece of rope, pieces of hair, feathers, and other unseen things woven into it. Its proximity to the fireplace makes it glow a faint red. I smile and put it back into my pocket. I didn't have to use it. Events didn't quite work out the way I or my associates had planned. Henry Nash and the agent and the actress were…regrettable, but necessary. Wheels are in motion. We just have to be patient. We can wait a bit longer.

*

Marshall

You can feel that the gloom has lifted. I'm still feeling tender from the gunshot wound, but there's the matter of the manager of the Cruthers.

"If you'll just settle our fee, we'll be on our way."

"Your fee? Your fee! For what? Half of my staff have left! When I find Eugene I'm going to kill him. So you can see that I have bigger fish to fry than you and your *fee*."

He turns his back on me, the cheeky fucker.

"You know that we solved your problem, right? If you haven't been up to floor six and a half yet, go up there: no flying chairs, and none of your staff are going to disappear and be replaced with a bomb blast. You're welcome. Now, pay up!"

He turns back around and gives me *that* slimy smile. "I don't know what you're talking about."

"Oh, I think you do. And we can easily reverse what we've done. Your choice."

Of course, there's no way we could—or would want to—reverse it, but Atherton doesn't know that.

He thinks for a moment. "Come with me."

Minutes later, we leave *considerably* better off than we were. I think he's sweetened it a bit just to get rid of us. We get that a lot.

We're approached by Murray. I'm a little wary—so far, she's either been arresting us or aiming a gun—but when I see who she's got with her I relax a bit. It's a dog of our acquaintance.

"Durham!" Conner yelps and runs up to the mutt, gets onto his knees, and scratches its head. Durham shakes his tail and licks Conner's nose, making him giggle. Shit, I can see which way this is going.

"Officer Murray—"

"It's *Detective* Murray. I thought you'd like to know that Phantoms Inc—" She stifles a laugh. "Sorry, that was a sneeze."

Yeah, sure.

"Anyway, yes, you and Conner are no longer people of interest in the recent murders."

"Well, that's a relief."

"The investigation is still open. We haven't been able to find Eugene or any members of the group known as the Infidels."

Funny that.

"Before you go and do whatever—"

"Voodoo that you do so well?"

"Don't push it."

"Fair point."

"Yes. Before you go, does this mean anything to you?"

Murray shows us a picture on her phone.

"Yes," I say, recognizing it from the picture Faulkmeyer showed us. "That's a Witch's Ladder. The Mescaleros used those in their rituals and as their calling card back in the day. Why?"

Murray is silent for a moment. "One each was found at three separate murder scenes: Angela Maron, Francis Goldstein and Henry Nash. Someone is sending us a message."

"Or a warning."

"What do you know about the Mescaleros?" she asks.

I get a shiver and look down at Conner, who momentarily stops fussing over Durham to look up at me.

"Not much," Conner lies, as he turns his attention back to our new friend.

Murray narrows her eyes.

I quickly jump in. "I can't tell you too much, but they appear to be a rival group to the Infidels."

"Oh yes? I'd be very interested to speak to them."

"So would we," I say.

"Hmm…In the meantime I need to find a home for this one," she says, looking down at Durham.

"Why, what were you thinking?" Conner asks.

"Dunno. Thought we'd have to take him to the animal care center."

"You can't do that!" He looks between me, Murray, and Durham.

"You can't be thinking…" I start.

"But look at him!" Conner ruffles the fur on Durham's face.

"He's such a good boy!"

"Jesus! Okay, let's see. But if Klaus…"

Murray moves to leave.

"Uh, before you go…Now that we're no longer persons of interest, have you thought about that Italian restaurant?"

"You're unbelievable!" She laughs.

I do a goofy shrug, which I hope is endearing.

"Huh, maybe. I've got your number, so I may give you a call sometime." She smiles and leaves.

May call you is better than a no. I look at Durham. What was I thinking? There's barely enough room for us in our office/apartment, let alone a dog.

To my surprise, Klaus is almost as taken with Durham as Conner is.

"Yeah, sure he can stay." He shrugs. "You pay the rent—most of the time."

"Ouch!"

He smiles. "It's your place, so as long as you take care of him and he doesn't get in the way…" He bends down and pats Durham's head. "Hell, I'll even take the dog for a walk for you now and then."

"Thanks Klaus. I guess we've got a new member of Phantoms Inc. Welcome to the team, pal!"

I lean down and our new joiner licks my nose. His breath smells of ass.

CHAPTER THIRTY

Marshall

"I'm exhausted." Conner looks at Durham. The enthusiasm at having a new dog friend has evaporated and left behind a tired nerd.

Before we take Durham up to his new home among the *Star Trek: Next Generation* tat in our office/apartment, we stop off at the bar in Donkey King. Conner has a Miller Lite—he doesn't drink often. I go for an IPA 'cause, despite it being a hipsters brew, I'm ashamed to say I've developed a taste for it. I get a bowl of water for Durham, who laps it up enthusiastically—man, that's one thirsty hound!

"You and Joey seemed to be on better terms," I say.

"Yes, no, well, we had to be. You know. We just talked. There's nothing in it. Why, what are you suggesting?"

"I'm not suggesting anything. You don't have to put your shield up with me, pal. I was just asking."

I look at him but he's looking at Durham.

"Is there anything I should know?" I ask.

"Like what?"

"I don't know; that's why I asked."

"No, no, everything's fine."

Hmmm. Conner's fine is very different to everyone else's.

We catch up on the rest of what happened while I was taking my nap in the forest, which sounds far more idyllic than it was. Conner stares at his drink through heavy-lidded eyes, and for a moment I think he's going to nod off, right there on the bar stool.

"You know when Han gets frozen in carbonite at the end of *Empire* and doesn't get defrosted until *Jedi*, three years later?"

I nod and he smiles.

"God, he must have felt *sooooo* rested," says Conner.

"Don't worry, with the money we got from Atherton we can afford to take a big glug of time off."

I open the door to our apartment and stare into the muzzle of a gun. Holding it is someone who I thought had died outside a secret base in Antarctica. A former client who double crossed us. Tania Voight is pointing a gun at us.

"I need your help."

COMING SOON!

Phantoms Inc will return *Phantoms Inc. Dance the Day of the Dead*, Halloween 2024.

*

SIGN UP!

For exclusive *'Phantoms Inc'* short stories and updates subscribe to out quarterly newsletter at:
www.phantomsincorporated.com

OTHER BOOKS IN THE PHANTOMS INC. SERIES:

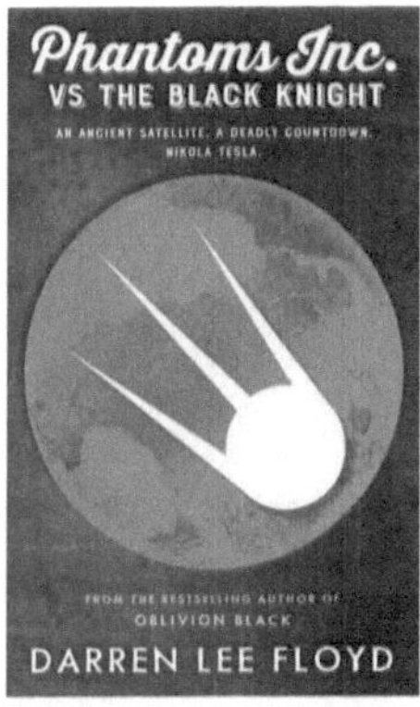

Conner Deal and Marshall Thompson of Phantoms Inc are 'ghost detectives'. Investigating hauntings and eerie events of all kinds, they uncover information from cold cases which elude traditional detectives.

While Conner has an intuitive grasp of everything technological, Marshall picks up echoes of past events from a myriad of objects and is even able to speak to the dead.

But no ghosts means no money. Phantoms Inc's finances are in a perilous state when Tania Voight walks into their lives. Regaling them with tales of her great grandfather's extraordinary work communicating with a mysterious ancient alien satellite dubbed 'The Black Knight' she makes a shocking revelation.

After 150 years of silence, the Black Knight has started transmitting again.

While tracking the coordinates of the transmissions to an abandoned Cold War base in Antarctica, Deal and Thompson also discover that others lurk in the shadows. A powerful, secretive organisation named Majestic 12 are trailing them, desperate to harness the satellite's power.

Reaching the frozen base, Deal and Thompson then make a horrifying discovery.

Something lurks beneath the ice and The Black Knight is about to awaken it.

"An appealing blend of noir detective and fantasy horror. Conner and Marshall investigate the coldest of cases..."

— Andrew Cartmel - author of
The Vinyl Detective books

"Supernatural meets Dr Who - only better... Well-crafted and full of twists. Quirky humour which keeps the reader grinning throughout..."

****** Amazon review*

ALSO BY
DARREN LEE FLOYD

A sanctuary built for the ultra elite to shield against the apocalypse.

Then the murders begin.

Something else is in there.

It always has been.

The best-selling *Oblivion Black* is available now, for Kindle and in paperback, on Amazon.

ACKNOWLEDGMENTS

Thanks to everyone at Stratopshere Books and to my editor Helen Woodhouse, to Kate Mattacks and Paul 'Captain' Kirkley for their eagle eyes. Finally thanks to Sian Floyd for her continued patience, love and support.

ABOUT THE AUTHOR

Darren formed the award winning RazorBlade Press in 1996. He ran the company for eight years publishing novels and a short story magazine.

Darren wrote and produced *'Anoraks'* a geek sitcom and had one of his short stories adapted for the stage by the Sherman Theatre.

His first novel - *'The Damage Done'* - was published by Headline in 1998. He has had four subsequent novels published.

His fourth novel - *'Oblivion Black'* - was published in 2020. It went on to become an international bestseller and has been adapted as an audiobook.

Darren is also a painter. He graduated with a B.A in Fine Art in 1995, has sold paintings to the Royal Academy and has had exhibitions in Cardiff, London and Bristol.

He lives in Cardiff with his wife and two cats.

www.darrenleefloyd.com